I0518817

Killer Bees

by Patrick MacAdoo

Killer Bees

© 2015 Nightman Publishing

This book is a work of fiction. Names, characters, businesses, organizations, places, events, and incidents either are the product of the author's imagination or are used fictitiously. Any resemblance to actual persons living, dead, or otherwise, events, or locales is entirely coincidental.

This book is protected under the copyright laws of the United States of America. Any reproduction or unauthorized use of the material or artwork contained herein is prohibited without the express written permission of the author or Nightman Publishing.

ISBN – 978-0-9909656-1-9

Printed in the United States of America

Chapter One

The flower's sticky, scratchy petals tickled Mikey's nose. The bright yellow bloom reminded him of breakfasttime before he started going to kindergarten, when they all used to eat together. Mommy always put fresh flowers on the kitchen table. He should've never left them. That's when Mommy and Daddy started getting mad at each other.

Mikey shaded his eyes. The sun was halfway up, the yellow flowers were opening all across the muskmelon fields. Pretty soon, Mommy and Daddy would wake up. He had to hurry. He didn't want to make them mad. He thought the trip would fix things. They pulled him out of kindergarten for a few weeks. Grampa, who especially made Mommy feel bad, stayed behind. But they fought about everything, dumb things like Daddy telling Mommy not to say 'global warming' in front of the Texans.

A *burring* bug grazed Mikey's head. He flinched and swiped at his ear, even though he knew better, he couldn't help it, the bug's big fat body freaking him out into forgetting what Daddy and Grampa told him about behaving around bees and other bugs. Sometimes Daddy and Grampa told him different things, and it was hard to remember what to do when only one of them was working around the hives, but it was worse when they were both around.

Be still.

The bug was the fattest bee he'd ever seen. The bee was so big he could see its rings, the yellows weird, bright and gross like a traffic light. He tracked the bee's loops and dives without moving a muscle, like Grampa told him to do when a bee was mad, it would've gone away by now if it wasn't mad, that's what Daddy always said, but Daddy also always said to not act scared.

The bee's wings buzzed louder than any bee he'd ever heard before, its swoops and dips were almost too fast for him to follow with his eyes. A bee thwacked onto the back of his wrist, making his forearm bob. He hissed in a sharp breath. The heavy bee crabbed itself around over his arm hairs until its long black feelers waved toward the flowers in his hand. Orange pollen crusted its bristly legs. Its stripes showed through its crinkly wings. A bee on his arm wouldn't bother him, even though this bee was the biggest he'd ever seen. He'd had bees on him lots of times, he'd even been stung a few times, it didn't even make him cry any more. But this bee's stinger was super-scary, long and jagged, and sharp on the tip, where a wet brown glob glistened.

Mikey opened his fist and let the flowers fall to the dirt. Another bee joined the flyer in zooming angry patterns around Mikey's head. The bee on his wrist shifted, drawing his attention. The bee bunched itself up, then darted backward, jabbing its stinger into Mikey's skin. The hurt rippled outward, rushing to the top of his skull, leaving goosebumps in its wake. Mikey yipped and swatted the bee before he could stop himself.

He blinked. His blow didn't squash the bee, but stunned it enough so that it dropped off his arm. The stinger quivered in his flesh. The hurt throbbed fresh pulses up his elbow and into his head. The stunned bee jittered in a circle on the dirt below. Mikey knew he'd done a bad thing. *Run!*

He dashed down the row, losing a sneaker in his headlong rush. Mommy would be mad, but the bees buzzed behind him, buzzed louder than his own panting. The camper was too far away, but he saw the shed he'd passed on the way, right on the edge of this field.

He tore across the rows in a straight line for the shed. The vines and creepers snatched at his feet. He stubbed his shoeless big toe on a hard stalk and stumbled, went down, skinning the heels of his palms and he plowed across the rows of low leafage. He bounded up and ran, he ducked as a swooping bee nicked his cheek.

He reached the old wooden shed and seized the door-clasp. The possibility that the door might be locked made his chest constrict. He yanked the rickety door open and howled his relief. He could hide here until Mommy and Daddy came. He surged inside and slammed the door shut behind himself. He huddled in the dark, wheezing giant breaths, inhaling the familiar smells of oil and gasoline.

Pock. Pock pock. The small bangs against the wooden walls increased, like that time that he and Grampa sat out on the screen porch and watched it hail. The bangs stopped. He rubbed his arm,

4

felt the stinger, and pulled it out. He realized that his arm didn't hurt, he couldn't feel it at all no matter how hard he rubbed it.

Bzzzzzzz.

Mikey froze. One had gotten inside, and was hovering overhead.

Chapter Two

The hard seat of the folding metal chair grated against Al's rump bone. He shifted and bumped his elbow into his right-hand neighbor's forearm. He mumbled, "Sorry," then softer he said, "Assholes." He glanced at his watch, then resumed staring at the stage. From above, florescent tubes spotlighted the imitation wood-grain podium, their glow decaying to a gray throughout the rest of the cramped 'event' room, the weak lighting matching the gloom of the thin industrial carpet.

Everybody knew the Southwestern Honeybee Collective was a sham organization set up by the pesticide companies to disseminate disinformation. The Collective's selection of this remote airport hotel for the site of their 'conference' proved their disdain for real beekeepers, and their selection for keynote speaker proved their real agenda, to discredit the current pesticide-fueled catastrophe. He bet the organizers were sweating bullets now, after he'd set up a flashmob-style invasion of this little conference, angry beekeepers packing the tiny room, a disturbance that was certain to end up on the local news. He hoped it'd go viral, expose the sleazy bastards once and for all, and especially the sleaziest of the bastards, Doctor Dean Hennig. Al curled his hands into tight fists.

Her intense scrutiny flared, scorched his left side. He uncurled his fists. He didn't need to look to know his wife's expression. The severe topknot of her sandy blonde locks bared her entire, makeup-free face. Her scowl crinkled her forehead and wrinkled the skin at the corners of her reddened eyes. Her lips compressed to pale slashes. At twenty-six, her skin still retained enough youthful freshness to bounce back, but he saw her bitchy glower as a preview of what he had to look forward to, should their marriage continue to limp along. With her arms folded tight across her breasts and her legs crossed, she managed to squeeze her long, full body into the tiny space afforded without so much as grazing him. She should've stayed in the motel room that they really couldn't afford, but she just had to be here, she couldn't let him out of her sight.

Al clasped his hands in his lap, but he couldn't help clamping them a bit. She blamed him. The rigid welts on Mikey's face, the way his little body jerked lifeless under Al's frantic efforts at CPR in that dim tool shed … Al closed his eyes. According to her sophomore-level psychoanalysis, he wasn't expressing enough grief. According to her amateur opinion, he was mimicking his old man's repressed stoicism. *Bullshit.* Just because he wasn't starting pointless arguments, like about an hour ago, insisting that they should go home, then conceding that they couldn't afford to take the loss, then using that fact to get in some digs about how he screwed up their finances, just because he wasn't acting batshit crazy didn't mean … He exhaled a slow breath, opening his eyes on the last wisps. He wasn't about to let her distract him. Not now.

From the corner of his eye he detected her trademark head-bow, its excruciating pace the only difference from her standard signal that she wanted to go, *immediately*. He grimaced. He ought to grant her wish, he ought to take her straight back to the motel room and have it out with her once and for all, something they should've done a long time ago, clear the air about everything, their marriage, the business, his old man, if they'd sucked it up and done it right when it needed doing, maybe Mikey would still be alive.

A squeal of electronic feedback drew Al's attention towards the stage. The Collective's president mumbled through an amplified, but sheepish introduction. Al guessed the asshole emcee was more than a bit embarrassed about how his little tea party got out of hand. Hennig's appearance on the left wing of the stage stirred a smattering of applause, which the boos quickly engulfed. The hostile reception didn't seem to fluster Hennig. His expensive dark suit swished back and forth from his thin, shortish frame as he took a slow, cocky stroll along the stage. He moved easy for a forty-five year old man, probably because he never put in an honest day's work his whole pampered life. Al was a decade younger, but every morning he woke up tight and sore from head to toe, a catalogue of minor repetitive-stress injuries dogging him. Even now his knees were beginning to throb from wedging himself into the cramped seating.

Hennig smiled while gripping the emcee's hand, then he stepped behind the podium and faced the crowd. The florescent light flashed off his bald crown and highlighted the reddish bristles horseshoeing his head, and reflected off the lenses of his black-framed spectacles. Hennig's thin lips curved into smug grin. Al sneered. Hennig was the enemy's mouthpiece. The bastard got himself appointed to the government's blue-ribbon committee on CCD and ever since had been steering the project into conclusions favorable to the big pesticide companies, the same tactics that Hennig, a darling of rightwing radio, had been practicing for years. He was their go-to expert for global-warming debunking. Who better to spearhead the charge to convince morons that Colony-Collapse Disorder was a myth? And Hennig had been beyond effective, one of the few things that Al and his old man agreed on, although Al suspected that the old man relished another reason to be disappointed in his always-disappointing son, another failure to pile on top of the others, like his failure to control his wife, and the looming failure to save the family business, and his failure to keep his son alive, and his failure to keep from bawling like a baby in front of God and everybody. Al sniffled as quietly as he could. His field of vision went shimmery.

Hennig launched into his speech. His prickish tone dried the mist from Al's eyes. Al tuned out the words. He'd heard Hennig make this same argument dozens of times, about how CCD had nothing to do with pesticides, but rather was the result of the unsustainable practices of commercial beekeepers. Hennig would cite such factors as fatigue caused by overuse, the stress of travel, the poor diet for bees subjected to monoculture, among others, all things that were authentic stresses on hives, and that was exactly why the bastard was so goddamned persuasive. Al sat up straight.

His scalp tingled. He knew everybody was looking at him, waiting for him to stand up. The tingle reminded him of high school, when the team looked to its starting quarterback to speak up to the coach about some shared concern, like increasing the frequency of water breaks. The concerns of the loose coalition of beekeepers he'd put together via the Internet weighed a little heavier on him. For months he'd been working on his refutation to Hennig's set speech, talking-point by talking-point. He'd been lying in wait for just this chance. He'd only get one shot at putting Hennig in his place.

He glanced at Sandy, then returned to staring at Hennig. *Obsessed.* Sandy used that word a lot ever since she went back to college. Obsessed with saving the family business in order to secure his father's approval, that's what drove him to work so hard to keep the business afloat, and to work so hard to draw together and lead a

8

resistance against the big pesticide machine, his obsession draining him, leaving very little left over for his family. He shook his head. That was more of her half-assed Psychology 101 bullshit. CCD was real, and it threatened the whole industry, and the family business, which in turn threatened his family, and that's why he worked so damned hard. She was the one drawing away, going to college, spending all her time in her 'study' doing homework, making whispered phone calls …

He didn't look at her, but he knew she was fuming, repeating in her head that the fact that he was sitting here was proof that being a bigshot was more important than his family. He ought to grab her and take her back to the motel and have it out with her. Just to show her that he was willing to sacrifice perhaps his one and only shot at confronting that bastard Hennig in public. Just to show her that family was the most important thing to him. But he could see his old man shaking his head, claiming that Sandy wore the pants, making Al give up his one chance to set things right in order to engage in some womanish foolishness that he could deal with any time at all. Al narrowed his eyes. His old man was wrong about so many things, but he'd be right about this. He stood up and strode towards the stage. He savored the uproar and Hennig's pregnant pause.

Oh god please sit down!

Al, stalking towards the stage, shouted, "So it's all our fault?"

Sandy grimaced. Her husband's raw tone foreboded a grief-fueled explosion.

"I didn't say that," Hennig said.

Al's gait lengthened, accelerated. Sandy marked the upward tilt of his head. She didn't need to see his face to know that he was aiming his lantern jaw at Hennig like a weapon. Al meant to put the little blowhard in his place. Apparently, he had forgotten that Hennig did this sort of thing for a living. A miraculous victory only would stiffen his resolve to remain on the road all the way to Central Valley, instead of going home, like they should.

"But that's what you mean," Al said. His voice deepened as he said, "Maybe it's not 'all,' but it's also next-generation nosema and varroa destructor, new versions of foulbrood and chalkbrood, hell, your cohorts have even blamed cell-phone towers, until their corporate masters told them to knock if off."

Al halted. The glow spotlighting the podium gleamed off his black hair, which was too shaggy for a man in his mid-thirties. Al squared his broad shoulders and said, "Why not blame UFO's?"

Sandy groaned. Al's quip scored some laughs. Hennig's loose suit ruffled, signifying a slight shift of body weight from one foot to the other, also signifying, Sandy knew from her course in body language, that Al's barb had ruffled Hennig's corporate cool. But the irony of Al's joke was not lost on Sandy. Her husband had been spiraling downward into a morass of conspiracy theories for years now. Should Al manage to knock Hennig back on his heels, well, that would be all the David-versus-Goliath inspiration he'd need to stay on the road. She foresaw long miles of silence in the truck's cab, Al's grim determination buffering and repressing his grief. He would refuse to talk about Mikey. She could ride with Sven, but dumping her despair on their lone remaining employee wouldn't be fair. Living with Al and his father on the remote farm had left her more than half-estranged from her brother and sister. She couldn't bring herself to call them out of the blue in a time of crisis, not when she hadn't been there for them, crises or not. The farm had also isolated her from her old friends, whom she'd lost touch with one by one. She couldn't imagine burdening her college acquaintances. The quixotic quest to save the family business would consume Al. His father hardly looked at her, much less deigned to speak to her. *That damned farm.* For a long time she'd been laying the groundwork to escape, all the while girding herself for the battle to take Mikey with her. But now that her dear child was gone, that damned farm was the only thing that offered her any comfort at all, the comfort of familiar surroundings, and she needed comfort. She couldn't leave Al right now anyways.

"You blame everything but pesticides," Al said. "What about neonicotinoids? What about the effects of stacking?"

"There is no research supporting–"

"That's the problem! There's no research at all! But go ahead an spray the crops with some newfangled pesticide, and go ahead and drench your crops with insecticides, herbicides, and fungicides at the same time, and damn the consequences!"

"That's not true ..."

10

"It isn't true, is it? There's been some research, the USAD have conducted their own studies, which, despite your best efforts to suppress, have leaked out, and what do these studies say?"

Sandy, realizing her mouth was hanging open, snapped her jaw shut. Al hadn't been this lucid, this sharp, since, well, she couldn't remember.

"They cite a number of factors," Hennig said.

"They cite pesticides. Then, what do you do? You attack the methodology of the research!"

"There were some, ah …" Hennig paused, his lips parted, appearing to struggle for the right words, then he resumed his reasonable tone, saying, "potential inconsistencies with the data collection and analysis."

Sandy leaned forward. *Keep the pressure on. Don't give the bastard time to slip away.*

"Kind'a stuff that's too complicated for a bunch of dimwitted beekeepers to understand, right?"

"Well, no …"

Al waved his hand. "Forget about all that stuff. What I'd like to hear you answer, and I'm sure everybody in this room would like to hear you answer, is, what about the French situation?"

A few *yeah*'s, and *damn-right*'s arose from the audience. Sandy squinted. She thought she detected the barest hint of a crease on Hennig's otherwise placid forehead.

"Ten years ago they suffered their own form of CCD," Al said. "Then they banned Gaucho, and problem solved. What do you have to say about that?"

Sandy reclined against her chair's metal back. Maybe she'd been wrong. Maybe attending this conference was a good thing. Maybe Al needed to get this stuff off his chest before he could move on to proper grieving.

"That case has no bearing on the present," Hennig said. "Different products, different region, different conditions, the events you describe happened over ten years ago. That's like comparing the dark ages to the digital revolution, in terms of the speed of technological advances!"

Al reared up to his full height, his boots' heels putting him a bit over six feet tall. His back straight, his large hands dangling loose at his sides, the stagelights limning his still-strong body with a nimbus of bright confidence, goosebumps broke out on her arms. He hadn't given her goosebumps since … since the night he, the hometown hero, proposed to her. Maybe standing up for what was right was his way of honoring their son's memory. She unfolded her arms and gripped the sides of her chair. *Just knock down his talking points, then finish him off.*

Al tilted his head to the side. *Don't say it!* He said, "Figures you'd say that." Sandy sagged. That hateful phrase, always the preamble to one of his pet conspiracy theories. She knew that his eyes flicked from side to side when he said, "Isn't it true that you own the majority stake in a company that imports foreign bees?"

Sandy spotted the upward twitch on the left side of Hennig's otherwise unsmiling lips. He was prepared for this accusation, no doubt, probably had been hoping for it. "That is true," Hennig said, "I do."

Al allowed the small flurry of crowd whispers to die out, then he said, "So you stand to benefit financially, if CCD wipes out American bees."

Hennig didn't have to wait as long for the crowd to quiet. "I suppose a pessimist, a doom-crier, a Chicken Little would interpret it so. But I bought shares in that particular brokerage company in order to regulate the flow of foreign bees onto the continent, to prevent the introduction of foreign diseases, while at the same time conducting research on a broad swath of specimens from around the world, in order to improve the American Honeybee."

Al snorted. "I suppose you're gonna tell us that's why the company that employs you bought the last company that did independent research on CCD."

Sandy winced despite the sporadic *yeah*'s supporting Al. Hennig was pulling Al's strings so well that Al didn't even feel it. The doctor spread his hands wide. "They did so on my recommendation."

A whine tainted Al's growl as he said, "So you admit it!"

"Of course. This pertains to our qualms concerning methodology. If anything, we've strengthened that company, updating their facilities, increasing their budget, broadening their purview, and thus, *increasing* their independence."

Al froze, than managed a scoff. "That's bullshit." His resorting to swearing made Sandy bow her head. "You just want to control the research, quash reports that damage the profits of your corporate overlords."

Sandy raised her eyes in time to catch the end of Hennig's sad shake of his head. "It is true that corporations are chiefly concerned with profits. There is no debating this. But my employers are not so shortsighted as you would wish. In the name of long-term profits, it is in my employers best interest to get to the bottom of CCD, whether or not it exists, and what can be done to combat it, should it exist."

"You know that's bullshit! You work for the pesticide companies, but you're on the government committee investigating CCD! That's a clear conflict of interest! They pay you to say nothing bad about pesticides, ever! And they pay you to make sure that the committee doesn't say anything bad about pesticides! If your corporate masters were killing babies, you'd still advocate for them, and probably put blame on the babies!"

"Wow." Hennig touched his temple, then dropped his hand. "It sounds more like *you're* unwilling to say anything good about the industry. It's simple math. No bees means no crops, no crops means no pesticides, herbicides, fungicides, which in turn means, no industry, no profits."

Hennig let his words sink in for a moment, then he clasped his hands behind his back. "Let's just cool down for a moment and look at it from a practical point of view. We live in a brave new world. Factory farms, monoculture, genetically modified crops, the list goes on. Whether CCD exists or is just an aggregate of smaller catastrophes does not really matter. What matters is, will we adapt? What we need is to keep up with the speed of technology. What we need is to nurture our bees to withstand the inevitable changes to their environment. Some," Hennig swept his right hand towards Al, "are entrenched in the past, and those that refuse to adapt will perish." Hennig rested the edge of his hand against his breast. "I, however, choose to believe that we are smart enough, capable enough, and good enough, to develop bees that will thrive in twenty-first century! I, for one, believe in American ingenuity. We shall adapt, and we shall ride ..."

Sandy tuned out, and anyways, the eruption of applause drowned out the last lines of his rousing call to action. Al slouched, seemed shrunken, totally destroyed. Tears blurred her vision. He didn't need this, this was the last thing he needed. She wiped her eyes, sniffled, and thought that the silver lining was that at least now he would be too embarrassed to show his face among his peers, and that at long last, they would go home.

Chapter Three

"We're two days late," Sandy said.

A day and half. Al clamped his molars down on the sides of his tongue. She knew he'd already called Billy Bob, she knew their plot was already secured. They'd have to bust ass, work around the clock, but they weren't too late, no matter how much she'd love them to be.

He shifted gears as they left the plateau and entered the last long rise. The green blur outside his window separated into individual firs. As the big rig labored up the steepening incline, the draft of crisp air through his open window flagged, leaving him exposed to the fury baking towards him from the passenger seat. Christ, it'd be nice if she'd let up on the bitchery for even a second.

A bone-jarring shudder oscillated through the truck's chassis. Squeaks and metallic squeals sounded from all over the cab. A pang spasmed low in Al's guts. The truck was falling apart.

"The truck's falling apart," Sandy said.

He sucked his upper lip between his teeth and bit down. She knew exactly what he was thinking, she knew exactly how to get his goat. They'd been over it a thousand times, that they didn't have the spare cash, let alone the spare time, to fix either truck, but she couldn't let pass an opportunity to remind him how much of a failure he was. If either truck broke down, then the business was finished, and wouldn't she love that.

He tried to pitch his voice breezy in order to avoid escalating their terse responses into an argument, but his tone sounded tight-jawed to him when he said, while patting the outside of the door with his left hand, "She just needs to make it a little bit farther."

"I just wanna take a shower."

He puffed a silent sigh out of the left corner of his mouth. She was probing for another way ignite the same old fight. No money to fix the trucks meant no money for hotels, which meant bunking in the trucks, and washing up at rest-stops and filling-station restrooms. Those slapdash sink-baths provided only superficial relief from the roadtrip grime, before the sun beating through the windshield restored the sweaty sheen that trapped the airborne particulates gushing in the open windows, which he supposed was also his fault since the air conditioner didn't work in either truck. Hot, sticky, miserable, like everything else, the decaying trucks, the tanking business, their crumbling marriage, everything was his fault, even ...

The truck crested the rise. As always, the pink-tinged white panorama of Central Valley's blossoming almond orchards took his breath away. In years past, he sometimes pulled the truck over and gawked. He'd planned to this year, to share this wonder. A heaviness descended upon his eyelids. He shifted, kept his foot off the brakes.

Tires screamed against the pavement. His eyes jerked from the side mirror to the rearview. The rig behind them veered, seemed on the verge of buckling, then performed a long convulsing skid before coming to a stop slantwise, its nose on the shoulder, the trailor still on the road.

Al pulled their truck over while Sandy tried to contact Sven on the CB. Once stopped, they jumped out of the truck and sprinted towards Sven's cab. They found the lanky Swede slumped behind the wheel, his blonde head lolling. They dragged Sven out of the cab and laid him out on the roadside grass. Al couldn't miss the welt to the left of Sven's jugular. The jagged black stinger bobbing from the middle of that angry red lump chilled him. He rasped, "Call 911."

Al scraped his fingernail against the stinger, which gouged the ridge of his nail before he dislodged the miniature harpoon. He flicked the sticky black weapon onto the grass. He dashed back to the truck and retrieved the first aid kit. By the time he returned, Sandy was on her knees beside Sven. Without looking at Al, she said, "Ambulance is on the way. I think he's in shock."

Neither of them said anything about the hundreds of stings Sven had endured in his career as a beekeeper. Al knelt beside Sven and swabbed the sting with alcohol, then popped the icepack and pressed it over the welt.

"How can he be allergic?" Sandy asked.

"He can't be." But Sven was pale, short of breath, his pulse crazy fast, and unconscious. Al was no doctor but he knew exactly what anaphylactic shock looked like, and it looked exactly like this.

Al gestured for Sandy to hold the icepack steady. He lurched to his feet and rushed toward Sven's cab. He scanned the cracked seats for any sign of Sven's attacker. Before ... they didn't find a single bee. He snatched up the pair of work gloves wedged between

16

the gear box and the driver's seat. Gloved, he sprawled over the seats and felt over the floorboards.

"What are we gonna do?"

He winced. For all they knew, Sven could die, and she was already jumping to how they'd be forced to pack it in without him.

"If we have to, we'll go it alone."

She huffed, just loud enough so he would hear her. He wanted to scream at her that he wanted to go home too, but they had no choice but to press on, they needed that six figure check. At least her growing bitchiness assured him that Sven was stabilizing.

Underneath the passenger seat, Al felt a weak wriggling against his gloved fingers. He got a gentle grip on the bee and drew the creature into the light. He whispered, "Oh Hell ..."

"What is it?"

He gaped at the stunted albino that crawled a twitchy, broke-leg circle in his palm.

"What, what is it?"

He couldn't find the breath to answer. He mouthed, 'CCD.'

Chapter Four

Al stooped over the hive body. He'd stopped bending his knees a while ago. Sandy had marked his gradual withdrawal from back-protecting technique. He was dog tired, but he refused to stop until he'd inspected every tray.

She bent her torso over the top of an already inspected hive-body, propping herself on her elbows against the hive's flat wooden top. She had to resist the urge to shuck the strips of peeling white paint, just like she had to resist the urge to warn him about his bad posture.

A runnel of sweat trickled down her temple. The veil, the suit, both at least three generations behind as far as cutting-edge tech went, amplified the already hot, bright afternoon's temp, despite the deep shade of orchard. She'd hadn't been outside the suit since she donned it at daybreak. Her own musk had deadened her sense of smell around noon.

Al's hunched back strained against the material of his suit. The white expanse showed faded black oil and green grass streaks, as well as the sutures where he'd sewn numerous gashes. Barehanded, Al jiggled another wooden tray from the hive body. He leaned close to the honeycomb.

"I wish you'd wear gloves." She bit her tongue, wishing she hadn't sounded so bitchy.

He muttered, "I need my hands free." He eased the tray back into the hive body, and moved on to the next one.

"Sven's been stung as much as you have. One sting put him flat on his back."

Gripping the tray, his knuckles turned white. He kept his head down. Once again, he ignored a prompt to discuss the connection between Sven's sting and Mikey's death. She couldn't even get him to utter Mikey's name. But she'd seen that wicked stinger too, and whatever species of bee had stung Sven, it sure as heck wasn't one of their gentle honeybees. Al'd overnighted the stinger to the medical examiner back in Texas, but they'd yet to hear back whether or not the stinger matched the dozens removed from Mikey. She didn't doubt that the stinger would match, but she feared the disinterest of the hospital administrators, who probably already ordered the disposal of the stinger samples. Not that positive confirmation would bring Mikey back, but they would know that at least one of the lethal bees had stowed away on their truck. He really should be wearing gloves.

"I need free hands for my system."

Her lips twitched. Him and his damned systems. His current system, like the vast majority of them, relegated her to the sidelines, useless and watching, while he took on the whole crushing workload himself. Trying to guilt her. Trying to impress daddy with his grace under pressure. Trying to work himself to the point of utter exhaustion so he wouldn't have to deal with his grief. So he wouldn't have to talk to her about their horrible loss, so they couldn't help each other, which left her drowning in the black depths of her own grief. With conscious effort, she unclenched her jaw. She didn't know if she should keep pushing him or if it'd be better to let him be. Either way, she couldn't leave him now. "Maybe Billy Bob knows a hand looking for some extra work."

"Everybody's already hired. Couldn't afford it anyways, especially after the fucker deducted the cost of the tarps."

She gazed towards the horizon. The thick pinkish-white flowering prevented her from seeing the tarps that boxed them in. The blue treetop-to-ground screens were Billy Bob's solution to the protests of the neighboring beekeepers. Somehow, word of the crippled, mutated bee found in Sven's cab had gotten around, and the possibility of CCD contamination freaked them all out. Billy Bob reassigned Al to an outlying plot and quarantined his bees, a compromise that quieted most of the assholes.

"Everybody's against me."

She'd heard that bitter tone before. He would not stop, come Hell or high water. She shivered. Once she worked up the nerve to tell him she was leaving, he might react the same way. He might refuse to sign the papers. Maybe he'd go nuts, stalk her, become violent … She gave her head a tiny shake. His family's way was to withdraw, to go ice cold. He might follow her, watch her, and he probably would refuse to sign the papers, trap her in separation limbo. But he would never hit her. She said, "I'm not."

"Bullshit."

She winced. She opened her mouth to protest, but she couldn't spit a word out. She couldn't deny it. He fails, they go home, it was simple math, and he knew she wanted to go home because he'd finally intuited that she planned on leaving him, and he understood that she couldn't while they were on the road.

"You want me to fail more than anybody, *now*."

Oh my god! She placed her palm against her veil so that the meshwork grazed her cheek. She had it all wrong. That 'now,' as close as he would come to saying anything about Mikey out loud, meant he believed that she blamed him. He believed she wanted him to fail because the family business had killed Mikey. He'd insisted that Mikey go on the road and begin learning the ropes. So it was his fault that Mikey had been there that awful day, and so, to his grief-stricken mind, it was his fault that Mikey was dead. She couldn't let him go on believing that she blamed him. She took a deep breath.

He said, "I know you just *loved* what happened at the conference."

She snapped her mouth shut.

His voice pitched into his conspiracy-theory tone, that whiney tone she hated so much, while he said, "You've been rooting against me all along. You're worse than useless. Why don't you just get the fuck out'a here?"

She jerked upright. She balled her fists. She'd done everything she could think of to help him deal with the workload. She'd backed him up all the goddamned way.

He twisted his neck so that his head angled in profile to her. His eye glittered red through the white veil. "Go!"

"Fine!" She spun and stomped away from him. She'd cleared their dumpy campground before her fury abated enough for her to think straight. If he didn't try to stop her, she'd get on a bus and this'd be the last damned time he ever saw her.

Chapter Five

Al shuttled the final tray home. He sighed. No sign of CCD. His spine crackled as he straightened from his hunch. He gazed the way she'd stormed. He sighed again, this time with no trace of relief. She'd stamped off in the exact opposite direction of the nearest road. He'd better go after her, if only to point her in the right direction.

Through the veil, he rubbed his forehead. *Christ, I'm an asshole.*

He shucked his protective suit. He started after her, angling westward through the orchard's rows. She must be royally pissed, walking away without any of her stuff, no money, not even her phone.

He halted in the shade and inhaled the fragrance of the almond blossoms. She would come back after she realized she hadn't grabbed her stuff, after she'd cooled off. He didn't really look forward to catching up with her anyways, not when she was so furious.

The sun's underside was about a minute from grazing the western peaks. Night fell fast in the valley. If she got lost after dark, something bad could happen, and that would be his fault too.

A sharp ping grated his right hip with every step. He clamped his jaw against the pain. She had about a twenty-minute head start. She might've come to her senses and turned around already. He blasted a bitter snort. The way his luck was running, she was probably sprinting away from him.

His hamstrings threatened to snap with each stride. His low back burned. The last thing he needed was to go traipsing all over the goddamned countryside. Maybe that was her true purpose, to punish him. Maybe he deserved it.

His vision tunneled, black electric fuzz funneling inward. He left the range of the hives' humming and entered a silent zone. His footfalls seemed overloud. He extended his fingers, then balled them into fists, again, and again. The repetition helped him to keep his mind a blank, but the effect weakened with each iteration, and the swirling black fuzz ate away at his blankness.

He grunted his awareness outward and seized on the silence of the orchard. No birdsong, not a peep. Pesticides killed birds too, either by depriving them of their food source, or by direct poisoning. He'd been screaming, both online and in-person, that pesticides were the obvious cause of CCD. Maybe jealous beekeepers spread the rumors. He sneered. More likely pesticide-company operatives had planted the CCD bee in Sven's cab and had conducted a whisper campaign to discredit loudmouth Albert Rhodes to the idiots, and to make him a cautionary tale to the few possessing half a brain. He nodded.

He pushed through a row and spotted her white veil lying in the grass. He snatched it up. The rest of her bee suit littered the ground further up the row. He picked those pieces up too, and wadded them in his hands. He rubbed the slick texture of the nylon material. She seemed to have altered her course, keeping to this row. He hated to think what might happen if he lost her trail. This was migrant-worker country. Illegal-immigrant country. The workers endured horribly suffering. The dehumanization of Hispanics created an understandable backlash. If she stumbled upon a crew of illegals, who'd be at least half-drunk after a brutal day's work in the fields, they probably wouldn't think twice about raping a lone Gringa. They'd bury her deep, too, so there'd be no victim to report the crime. Or a cartel gang might find her. They'd also rape her, but instead of murdering her, they'd smuggle her south of the border and she'd spend the rest of her days in forced prostitution. He'd read the stories.

He bellowed her name, his voice going ragged as he extended the last syllable, his holler masking the buzz until a blink before the fat bee thwacked onto his left forearm. Bigger than a queen, she sure as hell wasn't one of his. So much for Billy Bob's precious tarps. Her antennae waved toward him, then she doddered a semicircle in his wiry black arm hair. A nasty stinger jutted from her oily yellow and black-striped abdomen.

A dead match.

He tensed, couldn't help it, then he coaxed himself to relax, to not give her any reason to attack. No sweat, he'd done this a million times. All he had to do was wait for her to circle again, flick her onto the grass, and stomp the living shit out of her. Then he'd have a specimen. Proof.

He breathed slow, in through his nose, out through his mouth. His heartbeat decelerated. He let Sandy's bee suit slip out of his grasp and pool at his boots. As the monster bee rotated, he shifted his forearm to a slight downward angle. He curled his right index finger behind his right thumb, as if signaling 'Okay.' He let the force of his restrained index finger build to maximum, then he eased his hand towards the bee.

He whispered, "Everything's okay. Don't fly away."

He released his index finger and his fingernail whacked the bee square in the head. The impact numbed the tip of his finger. The bee held on to his arm hair. Stunned, she wobbled, then reared up her abdomen.

He threw a frantic chop at her. The ridge of his hand caromed off the meat of his forearm and swatted her to the grass. He pistoned his boot heel onto her, again and again. Fatigue consumed his adrenaline rush, and he stopped. Panting, he searched his forearm. No sting, but a slick of bug juice reflected the sunlight.

A nosediving buzz froze him. The bee whapped onto his left deltoid, where the gauzy material of his worn tee-shirt covered his skin. He detected the harmonized drone of a sizable swarm, the drone growing louder.

Shit.

He glanced at her suit. He'd never squeeze into it in time. He batted the bee off his shoulder and ran. He cut through rows, hoping the foliage would slow down the swarm, but his harsh huffs were too loud in his ears to tell. He burst through a row and discovered a slender stream. Gasping, he knelt on its grassy bank and washed the bee's viscera off his arm. He doubted he was pheromone-free. He held his breath. The trees dampened the approaching grind's volume, but not its rage. The water looked deep enough. He was too tired to outrun the swarm, but he knew the legends, fools lying underwater, breathing through reeds, only to find the swarm patiently waiting hours later for their victims to resurface. But he was gassed. He could at least get his wind back.

He scrabbled along the bank to a stand of weeds. He ripped up a hollow, dead shoot. He tore the root end off and blew it clear while wading into the stream. He laid down on the stream's pebbly bed. The cool water was just deep enough for him to fully submerge himself. He dug the fingers of his left hand into the stream's bed to hold himself underwater.

Overhead, the wavery blue darkened. As the hovering mass thickened and blocked out the sunlight, his calm surprised him. Maybe because this was undeniable proof that somebody was out to get him. Nothing else could explain the appearance of these unique bees, in swarm numbers, in both Texas and California.

He sucked a breath through the shoot, which had already absorbed a good deal of water. He wished he hadn't dropped Sandy's suit. His stomach clenched. They might've already gotten Sandy. Through the shoot, he exhaled, "No."

His toes broke the surface. He regripped the riverbed and pulled himself back under. She hadn't answered his call. She would've realized she was going the wrong way, she would've turned back, and they would've run into each other, unless she lied splayed in the grass, her tongue lolling, welts mottling her smooth skin, jagged black stingers protruding from the welts, just like …

He gazed up at the undulating black cloud. So he'd lost everything. Absolutely everything. No matter how hard he worked, everything slipped through his fingers. Now it was just him and the old man.

He loosened his grip on the riverbed. All he had to do was let go. Surface. It would hurt like Hell, but then it would finally be over. His muscles and his joints relaxed. He released the riverbed. He drifted upward. His thighs and chin broke the surface. His right ear rose above the waterline.

The swarm's blood frenzy sounded like revving chainsaws, sounded a thousand times louder than any swarm he'd ever heard in his life. He glowered. What were the odds of two separate swarms? If the swarm had gotten her already, it probably would've spent its rage, or at least the soldier bees would be mostly stingerless.

He jerked his body back underwater. She was still out there, alive, most likely walking back, maybe not for him, but surely for her stuff, her phone, her money. If he let himself go, then they'd get her next.

A bee plugged the shoot. He blowgunned the shoot clear. He let the current take him downstream, inching along the bottom. There had to be a way out of this.

Chapter Six

Sandy's sore feet forced her to slow. The summer heat waned as the bottom edge of the sun dipped below the western range. For several minutes now she'd left the pinkish-white petals carpeting the ground under the almond trees, while she sought the warm sunlight striking the narrow green strip of grass marking the center of the rows.

She exhaled a puff of hot air. The temp wasn't the only thing cooling down. Each step was just one more she'd have to retrace in order to go back and get her stuff. It would be dark by the time she got back, and she figured she probably wouldn't have the guts to set out again. Heck, she might not ever work up the guts to leave him again.

The thought of confronting him caused her dull headache to flare. Her stomach growled. She suppressed a dry cough. The need for food and water alone impelled her to return. Maybe tonight she'd bite the bullet and sit him down, and even if he didn't want to talk, even if he didn't say a word, she'd spill everything.

Out of the corner of her eye, between tree trunks several rows to her left, she caught a swatch of glossy industrial white, which stood out against the pink-tinged background. She stopped. She held her breath. Somehow, he'd tracked her down, even got ahead of her. She stared at the white patch while taking a soft step in the opposite direction. She frowned. The white was stationary. Another beekeeper? Yeah, she'd been distracted, but she would've remembered passing through Billy Bob's treetop-to-ground tarps.

She rubbed her forehead. Maybe she'd pitched such a fit that she did storm through the tarps without registering them. She started off toward them. Didn't matter. They'd have water, food, maybe a spare nutrition bar. She accelerated. Maybe she could bum a ride to Billy Bob's, who could collect her stuff for her, and she wouldn't have to go back and eat humble pie. She could be on the road home in a matter of hours.

She ducked between trees. *Home.* The house would be quieter than this silent orchard. Al's father wouldn't speak one word to her, wouldn't deign to look at her, much less offer an iota of consolation, oh, but his every little motion would broadcast accusation and condemnation, blaming her for Mikey's death. She swiped away teardrops and slitted her eyes. She'd be out of that damned house and into a new apartment before Al got back.

She hailed the beekeepers. She bit back a nervous laugh at their startled swivel towards her. "Oh my god am I glad to see you guys!" She cautioned herself to not mention her name, not just yet, in case they were part of the group that was protesting Al's presence in the Valley. She kept her eyes open for bees. She wished she hadn't discarded her suit. "Don't worry, I'm used to being around hives."

The two beekeepers, one about her height, the other more than half a foot taller, remained motionless. Maybe they recognized her as the wife of the infamous Albert Rhodes. They stood in front of the backend of a golf cart-like vehicle. A rectangular white container rested on the vehicle's bed. The container's compactness, as well as its ceramic and stainless-steel material, delayed Sandy's recognition of the hive. Just the one half-size hive was nowhere near enough to pollinate one of the typical allotments.

The beekeepers' suits gleamed whiter than any she'd ever seen, without so much as a grass stain, including boots and gloves. Instead of gauzy veils draped over wide-brimmed hats, black-visored, cylindrical helmets protected their heads. Their outfits seemed more Hazmat than apiarist.

They continued to stand still. Sandy slowed her pace. She chided herself for Al-level paranoia, but she decided it wouldn't be prudent to get into a vehicle with these two strangers. She cleared her throat and said, "I'll owe you bigtime if you'd call Billy Bob to come pick me up."

A bee, a big one, a jumbo queen, she would've guessed, if it made any sense for a queen to be flying free from a commercial hive, buzzed past her. She froze close enough to hear the pneumatic breaths of the beekeepers, whose helmets shifted slightly while tracing the bee's looping flight pattern. In between her and the beekeepers, the bee landed on a bloom sprouting from a low-hanging branch. The bee rotated, investigating the bloom's inner recesses. The jagged black stinger clashed with the delicate petal's pinkish-white hue.

Sandy blinked. The beekeepers' visors centered on her. She spun and sprinted. Footsteps pounded the ground behind her, each

26

loping stride closing the gap. When the thick glove clamped onto her shoulder, she screamed.

Chapter Seven

Al's backside grazed along the stream's bed. The stream was widening, growing more shallow. Already he'd had to dig his fingers into the muck and push himself along before the weakening current caught him again. All the while, the roiling cloud of bees cast a chilling shadow on him. He'd discarded the shoot, which had become too waterlogged, and every time he raised his face to sneak a breath, a squadron peeled off from the frenzied mass and blitzed his nose and mouth.

A shiver oscillated through his body. He just had to hold on until sunset. The swarm would return to its hive before full dark. He hoped. But the stream's cool water coupled with the constant shade under the swarm to threaten to induce hypothermia. Of course that wouldn't matter if the stream got any more shallow.

He took a peek then ducked his head back beneath the waterline. His chest constricted. The stream branched ahead. He'd been dreading this possibility, and the likelihood that either branch would be too shallow to submerge him. He dug his fingers into the river bottom and halted his progress.

The swarm hovered over him, blocking out the waning sunlight. He gritted his teeth against another full-body shiver. Just a little while long–

An agonizing cramp wracked his left thigh. He thrashed and groaned. Emitting a tight-jawed whine, sending up a flurry of tiny bubbles, he regained control of his limbs. Going all the way back to his high-school baseball days, he'd never relieved one of these white-hot seizures in any other way except by standing up and walking it off.

He had to restrain himself from lurching to his feet. He gnashed his teeth. He screwed his eyes shut. In the blackness behind his eyelids, electric white images crackled and pulsed in the shape of his thigh muscle, the stringy, burrowing fibers flaring more violently with each throb.

He thrust his gaping mouth above the waterline and wheezed in a giant breath before submerging again. The pain intensified, scrambling his brain, permitting only the fugue that it was getting worse. He knew of no precedent for waiting it out.

He tried different positions, bending and pistoning his knee this way and that, he tried massaging the cramp, but it kept getting worse. He flung himself over onto his belly. He placed his palms against the river's bottom, then thrust himself up to his feet.

He staggered toward the shore, his impaired left leg refusing to coordinate with his right. The swarm's shredding outrage deafened him. He splashed out of the stream. His first few left-footed stamps sent tracers of static across his field of vision. The modest grade of the stream's bank put a drag on his clumsy bolt. Overeager outriders slammed into his back, but failed to secure purchase on his dripping shirt.

He surmounted the rise and raced toward the trees. He crashed through low branches, their whippets lashing his face and arms. His stutter-stepping gait transformed, the cramp relaxing, his muscles remembering their old athletic dash.

A bee buzzed his right ear. Another caromed off his right shoulder. They were faster. The trees might break up the swarm's mass, but a single sting took Sven down. His breaths started to go ragged. Spots swam into his peripheral vision. He veered down a row in order to gain a respite from the slowing branches.

He squinted. Ahead, the warped walls of a rickety wooden shack broke up the column of almond trees. He leaned into a burst, burning the last of his reserves. He reached the shack's door and found a rusty padlock securing the door's steel latch. He grabbed the padlock with both hands and wrenched backwards, tearing the entire latch off the rain-rotted door. He slammed the door behind himself. He sank to the dirt floor and panted in the dim interior. He hung his head between his knees. Stream water dripped from his hair and soggy shirt.

The pattering of bees against the shack's exterior resounded over his rasps. They mottled the shack's single window, further darkening the single room. He figured it was a only a matter of minutes before they found a way through the crumbling wood. He barked a bitter laugh at the irony.

He scrunched his eyes. He hugged himself tight, he flexed his abs as hard as he could. He willed a black void in his mind, which held steady, then flickered, then fell under the onslaught of his familiar list of failures. After he led the team to state in high school everybody said he only needed a little seasoning to make the Show, but then, in college, he discovered that he couldn't foul off even a mildly competent curveball. The big hometown hero had let everybody down. This first flop, as always, played in clear, excruciating slow-motion, but then setback after setback whipped by before decelerating into Hennig's humiliation of him in front of the beekeepers he meant to rally against the pesticide industry. A sob escaped his lips. Even if he managed to survive, the family business was doomed, and Sandy was gonna leave him, if she, out there somewhere, in the open, vulnerable, also survived.

He raised his head and growled to his feet. He ignored the swarm's manic buzzing. He chided himself for stupidity. There was a good reason this shack still took up valuable orchard-space. He kicked through the junk until he spotted the conical shape he was looking for. He snatched up the homemade smoker. A protective wire grid surrounded the tin tank. The stiff leather bellows, mounted on the side of the tank, worked fine. He checked the fuel. The wad of compressed cotton inspired him to bare his teeth. Not full, but maybe enough. The DIY-beekeeper had left an old Bic lying in the wadding. Al blew on his fingertips to make sure they were dry, and he flicked the lighter. On the second try, a flame sparked up and he lit the underside of the wad. While the wadding smoldered, he rooted around and dug up a pair of ratty, elbow-length gloves and a filthy hat with a torn veil.

"Better than nothing."

He donned the protective gear. He booted the shack's door open, wheeled, and let the swarm have it. Gray fumes agitated over the shack, scattering the swarm. He swept the smoker's spout in a Z-pattern while he back-peddled. He gazed north. He could run for the stream, cross it, maybe leave their territory, maybe they'd no longer consider him a threat.

The smoke's steady flow decayed to spurts. He flashed on his father. If the old man learned that Al had chickened out and left his wife to fend for herself …

He dropped the smoker and ran deeper into the orchard.

Chapter Eight

The setting sun rimmed the western range, purpling the sky. Al bent over, planting his palms on his kneecaps to take the weight of his torso. No trace of Sandy, he hadn't the foggiest idea where he was, but at least he appeared to have lost the bees.

He glared at the pinkish white carpet of fallen almond petals. The bees' size, the density of their swarm, the severity of the their stings, even their vivid coloring, were nothing like he'd ever encountered in his career. He couldn't discount the possibility that they might be nocturnal as well, that they might pick up his trail and harry him throughout the night.

He shoved his torso upright and started a slow turn. He needed shelter, food, water. He had to find somebody, he had to call in the authorities. He scanned the darkling orchard for any twinkle of light.

He halted. He hurried, wending through the maze of tree trunks, towards the disturbance in the otherwise unbroken snow-like strips under the shadows of the branches.

He skated to a stop at the edge of the disturbance. Torn and shredded petals bordered the patches of green grass splotching the pink-tinged white. He spotted a pair of old sneakers. He relaxed his jaw while exhaling his lungs empty. Back home, Sandy loved to kick off her shoes and walk barefoot in the grass, especially at the end of a long day of chores.

Preparing to holler her name, his breath caught mid-inhale. No matter how mad she was, she wouldn't have left her sneakers behind. The laces were still tied, as if her shoes were ripped away while she tried to fight off her abductors.

The deepening twilight thwarted his vision. He dropped to his knees and skimmed his palms over the ground. The grass blades and flower petals riffled against the webbing between his fingers.

Sharp metal pricked his finger. He snatched up the earring and dangled it before his eyes. Sandy always wore posts. He scrutinized the miniature gold butterfly. Tiny red stones decorated its wings. Sandy would never wear anything so girlish. He stared at the sneakers, which looked a little smallish for Sandy, then he looked at the ground. He imagined a pair of hormone-stricken teenagers who snuck out to a remote spot in the orchard for a romantic roll in the petals.

He sagged, then flopped to his backside. This was not a crime scene. He groaned, though, when he realized that he was no closer to finding her. His stomach rumbled. His throat scraped sandpaper dry. He supposed he could wring moisture out of his squishy socks. He wondered if she was out there somewhere, lost, like him, and so damned tired. His eyelids fluttered, then closed. He just needed to rest for a second. Best case, she was on a bus headed back home. Best case, all the work rested on his shoulders now, and after running all over the countryside, the wasted time, the wasted energy, and he still had to find his way back … that was the best case.

His nostrils flared. If she hadn't stormed off, none of this would be happening. But her lack of support, her dragging her heels all the way, maybe this was exactly what she wanted, him working alone, completely exhausted, making it nearly impossible to get this job done. Sabotage. He should be asleep, so that he'd wake up rested before dawn, ready to work, ready to get things back on track. He might be tucked in his sleeping bag in the trailer's living room while she slept in the bedroom, but she'd be safe. This was all her fault.

He rubbed his gritty forehead. *Christ I'm an asshole.* He mumbled, "No wonder she wants to leave me."

His chest bucked with the effort to choke down a sob. He opened his eyes. That was the first time he'd ever said it out loud. She was gonna leave him. Then it would be just him and the old man alone on the farm. The old man's eyes, darker, smaller, would always be accusing him …

He scrunched his eyes shut and pressed his palms to his eyelids, then slid them down his face and chest, and he mashed his hands against his stomach. He flexed his abs as hard as he could against the pressure.

He growled, then with a burst he sprawled his limbs wide and gulped air. She wasn't stupid. She wouldn't blunder out in the open, wouldn't be an easy mark for predators. She'd hide, she might be holed up right now, waiting for him, and if he could save her, he might win her back …

He rolled over onto his stomach. He lurched up to his hands and knees. He waited out a slight dizzy spell, which descended into a jagged hum. Too late, too slow, he grasped that the noise was outside of his brain. A bee thumped onto his shoulder and danced a manic circle. He lunged to his feet while slapping at the bee's heavy body. He managed to dislodge it, but another crash-landed onto his left wrist.

Agony rocketed up his forearm and blasted his consciousness to bits. He staggered to a knee. The pain radiated upwards in great wobbly pulses, then a tingly numbness oozed up his arm and swamped the rest of his body. His chin slacked. A rill of drool spilled over his lower lip. The ground yawed, became a pink, white, and green kaleidoscope. He clung to the terror that he was a sitting duck for the swarm, then even that disintegrated to vibrating particles.

Chapter Nine

Sandy's shoulders strained. Her burden overextended her arms so that they felt like they were gonna rip out of their sockets. Her sweaty palms kept slipping on the cool ceramic shell coating the pair of beer cooler-shaped containers, which, she judged by their heft, had to be made of metal. Back at the service road where they'd parked the cart, at the crack of dawn that now seemed a million miles ago, the shorter one had whispered something to the goon, who then warned her, in his rumbling and rushed, yet careful enunciation, 'You better not drop them.' They'd forced her to be their pack mule. She deduced that they meant to keep her too exhausted to think about trying to escape until they figured out what to do with her. She'd spent the night hogtied and locked inside a cramped closet. The spasms and pains flaring in her muscles and joints had jolted her out of the few shallow dozes she'd managed. They'd given her a glass of lukewarm water and a melty Snickers bar for breakfast, but that minor bump in energy was long gone.

From behind, the goon's heavy breaths invaded her personal space. She forced herself to quicken, despite the short cord joining her ankles and hampering her stride to a shuffle, before he could go for another groping shove. His black visor did nothing to disguise his obvious leers, his eyes crawling all over her body, lingering on her breasts. She used her disgust as fuel to hoist the containers a little higher, and to increase her speed.

The shorter one, striding in front of her, set a brisk pace while guiding their little party to … wherever. Like the goon, a pristine white, full-body bee suit protected the shorter one, his cylindrical helmet sealed to his suit's neck. She'd gleaned that the suits were temperature regulated, unlike her jeans and the smelly long-sleeved flannel shirt they'd given her. She'd stopped sweating a while ago. She guessed she was pretty deep into dehydration. Her skin felt arid, her clothing trapping the heat, but she didn't dare unbutton, given the Hazmat care their suits implied.

A small white tote swung under the shorter one's armpit, its strap over his left shoulder. With the boots and the supersized cylindrical helmet he stood taller than her, not really short at all, but estimated height wasn't enough to go on. She couldn't place his body language, but the trouble he took to prevent her from hearing his voice … he had to be afraid she would recognize him. They'd blindfolded her at times, at all other times they wore the helmets. She clung to their secrecy as proof that whatever they were doing, probably poaching given the recent honeybee shortages, the stakes weren't so high that they planned to murder her. She was betting that they'd leave her tied up along the roadside whenever they were done doing whatever they were doing.

The shorter one came to a halt and held up the back of his gloved hand. Beyond him, a pair of white boxes, hive bodies, sat in the grass between the rows of almond trees. Sandy judged by their size that each body contained about a half dozen hives. Wood showed through the chips and flakes in the white paint.

The shorter one pointed at the grass in front of the hive bodies. She shuffled over and placed the containers before the hives. As she backed up she shook feeling into her dead arms. She stepped too far and the hobbling cord tautened. She flailed for balance, but instinct forced another too-long step and she careened to her butt, skidding on the pink-tinted petals into the shade of the almond trees.

The goon's helmeted head tilted backward and his body quivered, no doubt laughing his ass off at her. The short one unzipped his tote. He removed a ceramic tube about the length of his forearm. An orb the size of a softball closed one end of the tube. He opened a tiny hatch on the orb and inserted something that Sandy couldn't make out, then he closed the hatch.

The goon slid the top tray partway out of one of the hive bodies. Neither of them seemed to be watching her. She leaned forward, toward her ankles, and began to pry at the clumsy, overdone knot securing the cord to her right ankle. The cord slackened a bit. She was farmgirl. She knew her knots.

The shorter one aimed the open end of the tube at the tray and pressed a button. With a pneumatic whoosh a spurt of smoke gushed into the hive. She frowned. She'd never heard of poachers smoking a hive. The easiest way was to set a hive trap nearby. Some assholes just stole queens. But mollifying the few bees that remained in the hive during pollination didn't make any sense.

She snapped out of it and went back to work on the knot. She didn't want to untie herself completely, instead she aimed to loosen it enough to kick free if things got hairy and she decided to make a break for it. She kept her eyes on the goon, who appeared engrossed with pulling out hive trays so that the shorter one could smoke the bees.

Without moving her head she switched her focus between the goon and each little subsection of the ground. She flexed her jaw against the rising disappointment. Not even a glint of metal. She guessed the beekeepers who ran this station weren't the type to leave tools laying around. She spotted the bole of branch breaking the surface of the blanketing petals, which obscured the branch's length. About as thick as the barrel of a baseball bat, there was no estimating rot or flimsiness. She returned her attention to her captors. Maybe she should just ride it out, they were probably gonna let her go. She didn't want to provoke them.

The shorter one inserted the tubular smoker back into the tote and zipped the bag shut. The duo shifted to the ceramic containers, then, in unison, performed a slow half-turn until their shiny black visors aimed at her. She took a deep breath through her nose. They continued to stare. *They knew.* Their unrelenting gaze impelled her to drop her head and stare the grass. The corner of her mouth twitched. She narrowed her eyes. *Assholes.*

In her peripheral, she detected motion. She looked up. The goon had pivoted into her eyeline, his back blocking her view of what the shorter one was doing, but the task seemed to require both men's total concentration. She craned her neck, bobbed from the left to the right, but she couldn't see around the goon's stooped back.

The shorter one held up a long, slender stainless steel pincer that tapered to delicate jaws that held the biggest queen bee she ever saw. Even from her distance she could tell the monstrous, squirming bee was a queen. *A killer queen.*

She tore the cord from her ankle and lunged to her feet. She feigned a stumble. She watched in her periphery for the goon's reaction. When he broke towards her, she veered toward the branch. As his footfalls approached, she scooped up the branch, which was heavier and longer than she'd hoped. She whirled.

The branch's weight resisted her torque, reducing her swing to a swat, then she shrieked, and generated more momentum. He anticipated the blow and twisted. The branch shattered against the side of his kneecap.

She dropped her half of the broken branch and surged away from him. Off balance, she stabbed her right palm into the petals and stabilized her body, firing her legs back underneath her torso. She glanced over her shoulder. The goon was down, gripping his kneecap. She accelerated to an all-out dash.

Between her huffs, a machine-like stamp battered the ground, louder and louder. She looked back. The shorter one, running like an Olympic sprinter, arms and legs nearly a blur, but his torso and head steady, caught her before her dismay could fully form, and he flung her to the grass.

She tumbled. She cried out as the world reeled. She banged her elbow against a hard root. She rolled to a rest flat on her back. She groaned. His silhouette loomed black against the sun. Not even a tiny bit winded, he said, "We'll require more secure bonds."

She recognized that oily, smug voice. She rasped, "No." She shaded her eyes. His thinning red hair was a little mussed, and he wasn't wearing glasses, but it was Doctor Dean Hennig.

Hennig nodded his head towards the goon, who limped into view, and he said, "Make another attempt, and I'll leave you alone with him tonight."

Chapter Ten

A ragged green loop slashed through the pinked whiteness. Al groaned. The grass bristling through the flaky expanse of petals marked his weaving shamble. He'd been walking in circles. He stopped in front of a tree and rested his forehead against its trunk. He closed his eyes. The moisture rimming his eyelids wobbled, threatened to coalesce into teardrops. His left knee hurt. A memory flickered, his kneecap banging into a windowsill as he clambered inside a darkened house. Then the glare of refrigerator light. Gulping cool, refreshing sweetness, and struggling for breath around his crammed-full mouth. Yells, dodging the beams of flashlights, a chuffing ramble into the deeper nighttime dark, reentering the orchards. Then nothing but his zombie-like meander through the maze of almond trees until sunrise.

He shoved away from the tree trunk. He swayed as static sizzled through his field of vision. He recalled a night filled with such headrushes. After this current spell fizzled, endless green and pinkish-white stretched in all directions.

His body's general numbness dissipated along with the rush. His hamstrings were sprung. His low back ached. He began a deep breath, but a sharp pang, erupting from the right side of his rib cage, stopped him. He massaged his abdomen. The sting on his wrist had faded from angry red to a brown knob. A dull ache banded across his forehead from temple to temple, an ache familiar from his college hangovers.

He shaded his eyes against the morning sun. He squinted. "Can't be."

He'd seen the twin-boled tree from the opposite side, when he'd gone with Billy Bob to reason with a protesting neighbor. The stooped and skinny asshole, tiny head, tiny eyes, a poseurish blond lock streaking his longish bangs, was one of the most vocal protesters against Rhodes' Bees' participation in the Chase. The asshole wouldn't listen, wouldn't stop bitching up a storm about CCD, and after a while, so he wouldn't knock the fucker's block off, Al had fixed his gaze on the mutant tree, so weird among the manicured rows, until Billy Bob had offered the solution of the tarps.

He staggered eastward. The tarps ought to be just beyond the next rise. With each step, despite the upslope's drag on his calves, the stiffness melted from his gait. Sandy was probably sitting outside the trailer, bare feet up and wriggling her toes, sipping lemonade in the shade, having finished the morning's chores. She was probably waiting to interrogate him about where he'd been all the live-long night.

His grin died at the crest of the rise. No tarps, no mini-maze of hives, no camps, no Sandy waiting for him at home base. Only almond trees. He imagined his neglected hives, the collective buzz of the trapped bees growing more and more agitated. She wasn't coming back. His eyes narrowed. She'd timed it so that she'd abandon him at the worst possible moment. Now, with the lost morning, and probably a lost day, her little scheme was coming to fruition. The business would fail. The old man would blame him, maybe even change his last will and testament, and leave the farm to her …

"Christ."

He rubbed his sweaty forehead, then ran his fingers through his dirty hair. She hadn't *timed* anything. He'd provoked her, knowing how raw she was. He was the asshole, he did it on purpose, he drove her away. The old man would be right to blame him. This was his all his fault, so it was up to him to fix it.

He hurried eastward. He had to contact the authorities, they had to start searching for her. If he kept to the sun, sooner or later he had to run into somebody with a phone.

A nearby buzz made him flinch. He dived to his belly. The bee droned overhead, away from him. He barked a nervous laugh. Of course bees were pollinating blossoms all over the place. He stood and spotted a squadron of honeybees skimming the trees' blossoms. He fingered the nubby sting on his wrist. If not for the welt, he could almost believe the whole swarm had been a hallucination brought on by stress, sleep-deprivation, dehydration, hunger, a perfect storm fueled by …

He trembled. He focused on the honeybees. He frowned. The clusters weren't landing, they weren't tasting the blossoms, they were zooming at top speed. A distorted grinding engulfed the thin buzz of the fleeing bees. He spun, stumbled, and a hail of monster bees drilled into him, slamming him to the ground. He screamed throughout the first burst of stings.

Chapter Eleven

The goon *scritched* out another length of duct tape, then gnawed its end free from the gray roll. He applied the strip to the thick wad bonding her wrists together. At least this time he didn't grope her, or rub his erection on her, his excitement obvious against the faded fabric of his jeans. He, like Hennig, had shucked the fancy bee suits for work boots, jeans, and tee-shirts. Ever since Hennig left to obtain more secure bonds, the goon's dull brown smallish eyes, appearing all the smaller due to his long nose and drooping jaw, had grown more and more glassy as he felt her up while duct-taping her ankles and wrists.

The goon flipped her onto her stomach. She gnashed her teeth. *Here it comes.* She'd wait for a good shot. Head butt, biting, whatever. Something that would ruin his memories of this violation.

His clodhoppers pounded away from her. She twisted her head towards him. His belt clasp jangled loose as he ducked behind a clump of head-high weeds. She doubted he was urinating behind that greenish-brown screen. Hennig must have forbade him from assaulting her. Probably holding out the possibility as a reward.

She growled while trying to wrench apart her wrists, but the layers of tape didn't give an inch. The effort sapped her exhausted shoulder muscles. With a groan, she let her arms collapse to the patchy grass. Hennig, before driving away from this desolate tract at the edge of a stunted plot of the orchard, had assured her that capturing her wasn't part of the plan. He'd promised to improvise a role for her that would leave her unharmed. The fact that he'd revealed himself to her suggested his promises were meant to keep her docile until he figured out the best way to murder her.

Like he murdered Mikey.

She gazed at the pair of stacked ceramic containers. They must confine the hives of the killer bees. He couldn't take them because he couldn't risk being caught with them. The killer bees' presence both down south and here in the Valley made sense now. She snorted. Al was actually right about the conspiracy against him.

She scanned the area for anything that might help her escape, but her gaze kept returning to the containers. She balled her fists as hard as she could, then she extended her fingers. *The idiot.* If she could open the containers, the bees would kill them all, now that their fancy suits weren't protecting them. She'd be dead too, and she'd never know if she got him, but she also didn't know if she'd get another shot at him before he killed her.

She dragged herself on her elbows and knees, inching across the dirt. Through the brown and pale green leaves and stalks, he glanced at her. She flopped onto her back and faked a moan, as if she was trying to get comfortable. She writhed. She snuck looks at him. He grunted, and grunted again, and again.

She flipped back to her stomach. Judging by the accelerating and deepening of his rasps, he wouldn't last much longer. The gravelly soil raked her through her shirt and jeans. The containers loomed. The cluster of weeds swished. She froze, then rolled herself, completing three revolutions before bumping the containers.

She held her breath, expecting to hear his stomps over her careening heartbeat. She scrabbled up to her knees and peered over the containers. Nothing. Nothing but his manic panting.

She rotated her bound wrists so that her right-hand fingers touched the latch. The stainless steel lever swiveled counterclockwise on its hub less than a centimeter and stopped. *Locked.*

She choked down a frustrated cry. She jiggled the lever back and forth. She wrenched it, but it was too sturdy to break. He uttered a long, shuddery sigh. Her frantic efforts caused the container to shift on top of the other.

Her eyes darted, her vision blurring from the latch to the weeds, from the weeds to the latch, he was gonna come running any second now … the button in the center of the lever's hub drew her attention. She muttered, "Christ."

She thumbed the button while twisting the lever, which allowed a half-turn. The clamp released the container's lid. She worked her fingers underneath the lid. This was gonna hurt like Hell. A low cry erupted from deep within her, its intensity astonishing her. Maybe her mother had been right all along, maybe she'd rejoin Mikey in Heaven. A cold smile flickered at the corners of her lips. Her mother's ilk claimed they didn't allow suicides past the Pearly Gates. She guessed that sin didn't matter so much considering she meant to murder two men, the same way the bastards murdered her son, who never did anything to anybody.

Her eyes widened. She let her fingers slip out from underneath the lid. If she released the bees, and they stung the three of them to death, there was no telling where it would end, especially with their keepers dead. Innocent migrant workers, other beekeepers, maybe even more children.

She scrutinized the infertile plot one last time for any means of escape.

"WHAT YOU DOING?"

The goon loped toward her, pulling his jeans up, trying to cinch his jangling belt, while repeating, in his clipped, deep voice, "What you doing! What you doing!"

He shoved her away from the containers. Her heavy thud into the dirt cut off her outraged scream. He leaned over her and pointed his long index finger at her. "I'm gonna tell!"

Chapter Twelve

Al lashed his arm toward a spiraling bee. He snapped his hand shut. He didn't see the bee winging an escape, but he couldn't feel it wriggling against his palm either. He couldn't feel his palm at all. He squeezed his fist. Cloudy juice oozed from between his fingers. He flicked the smooshed carcass to the grass. Dozens of flattened, black and radiation-yellow corpses marred the petal-strewn green.

A diving buzz made him flinch and cover his eyes. His grampa's chaw-slurred warning echoed in his head, 'If pissed bees ever swarm ya, curl up, and cover yer eyes!'

The bee circled back. He stood still, waiting, and when the big fucker hummed into range, with a "Hi-Yah!" he swatted it out of the air. The bee thumped into the grass. He stomped it, again and again, just to be sure, because he couldn't feel it beneath his sole, couldn't feel his insole beneath his foot, for that matter.

He whipped his head back and forth while his stuttering pulse seemed to bang against the inside of his skull. No flyers invaded the air space. He lurched from one wounded bee to another, stamping those that lied on their backs with their jointed black legs waving in the air, and those whose antennae gave so much as a single quiver. While crushing the survivors beneath his boot heel, he scraped jagged stingers out of the rigid red welts encrusting his bare arms and the back of his hands. Shreds, as well as a few entire bee corpses, smeared his shirt and jeans. Surveying the dead and the dying, he couldn't help wondering where the rest of them went. There seemed to be so many more.

A distant gunshot snatched his attention. *People*! He launched himself in the direction of the blast. His gait wobbled. His numbed feet and legs kept him from timing his footfalls' impact with the ground, and he stumbled and staggered, but he managed to bull through the willowy low branches between trees, and he always remembered to protect his eyes.

He burst into a row and skated across the slick petals to a stop. A dude pointed a shotgun at him. Behind the dude, three guys sat on the grass, their hands tied behind their backs.

Under the brim of his cowboy hat, the mustachioed dude's eyes bulged. He whispered, "Jesus fucking Christ." The dude dropped his shotgun and bolted. His cowboy boots clomped. The low branches knocked the hat off his head. Before he disappeared through the almond trees, the sunlight reflected off his bald spot.

Al bent down and scooped up the shotgun. On the way back up, fuzz percolated into his sight until the static struck him blind. Sharp, rapid-fire, indecipherable utterances strafed his ears. As his vision cleared, the racket modulated into harsh, whispered Spanish.

He lurched toward the captives. One sprang to his feet and dashed away, his hands still zip-tied behind his back, the tail of his flannel shirt flapping behind him before he disappeared into the trees.

Al swayed, then shrugged. He plunged to a knee behind one of the remaining captives, who flinched. The captive whimpered, tried to scooch away from Al, then, as Al grasped the plastic between the captive's wrists and fumbled with the tie, the man's tone transformed from terror to gratitude, although Al couldn't understand a word he said.

Al made eye contact with the other captive. "You see a white woman, tall, but not too tall … longish sandy-blonde hair … some meat on her bones, pretty?"

The other captive let out a torrent of Spanish.

Al frowned. "No comprendo, mi amigo."

The other captive continued his diatribe. Al focused on the zip-tie, but he couldn't figure out the trick. The other captive raised his voice to a near shout. He raised his leg off the ground and shook his boot at Al, who spotted the boot-sheath peaking out from under the cuff of the captive's jeans.

Al crawled over and unsheathed the buck knife. He returned to the first captive and sawed the dull blade into the plastic. "Who did this to you?" He couldn't decipher their run-on responses, but the presence of a cowboy guard pointed towards one particular asshole. *Billy Bob.* Al barked a sarcastic laugh. He'd done a little research on 'Billy Bob,' whose real name was Rochester Ignatius Willoughby. Billy Bob played at being a cowboy, but his family was northern and old money. He was exactly the kind of asshole who would work with the CIA. Everybody knew all about the CIA-backed smuggling routes. The Company's pipeline had been pumping cocaine from

Latin American into California since the Iran-Contra days. Back then, only Freeway Ricky Ross went to prison, and that meant the superstructure of the pipelines remained intact. Billy Bob worked as a broker for the Almond Chase for maybe a month out of the year. That left eleven months to supervise the operation.

The buck knife's blade split the plastic band. The freed man scrambled to his feet and dashed into the trees. Al didn't blame him. He moved onto the bonds of the last captive. Probably Billy Bob's thugs forced these poor shmucks to mule cocaine, then, once they crossed the border, the poor bastards made a break for it, immigrants chasing their American dream.

When Al cut the man loose, he tried to pull Al into the trees, while whispering, "Rapido, rapido!" His bloodshot eyes, the wrinkles creasing his forehead, his frantic tugs on Al's arm … maybe he'd better go with the man. Faded green marks marred the leathery back of the brown hand clutching his forearm. The marks joined in some glyph Al didn't recognize, but the cheap ink screamed 'Prison tat.'

Al scrutinized the man's yellowish eyes. Maybe he'd made a mistake, maybe the prisoners were criminals. Al blinked. No, a criminal wouldn't try to get him to run too. These guys were afraid that Billy Bob's men would execute them. He remembered the shotgun. He shook himself from the man and bent down. When he stood up, gun in hand, the man was already running. Al muttered, "Godspeed."

"There!"

Al swung around toward the shout. He caught snatches of alien color between the trees. He guessed four or five thugs, coming right for him. He wheeled and sped through a couple of rows before ducking behind a thick tree trunk. He held his breath.

He listened to their crashing through the foliage, their curses, all in English. He held the shotgun parallel to his body, and tried to be thin behind the tree trunk. When their footfalls trailed off in another direction, he let out a huge breath.

His eyes flicked back and forth. He ducked low and crept, following in their wake. They would lead him straight to Billy Bob, who probably kidnapped Sandy, meaning to sell her into slavery. His eyes narrowed. Or maybe the old pervert meant to keep her for himself. He remembered the way the skeevy old motherfucker used

46

to leer at her. He would rescue Sandy, and expose Billy Bob once and for all.

Chapter Thirteen

Al kept to the edges of the woods, the almond trees giving way to pine the last quarter mile or so as he tracked the cowboys to what had to be Billy Bob's headquarters. Maybe a dozen big-honkin, shiny pickups, parked helter-skelter, crowded the dirt in front of the log cabin. At least two dozen cowboys, all of them toting shotguns or AK's, milled around the cabin's porch.

Al itched his left forearm. He couldn't feel his ragged fingernails scraping his skin, so he bore down harder until his scratches pierced the numbness. The warmth gratified him, then a bolt of agony stabbed up from his left thigh and forced a low whine, which escaped through his gritted teeth. The rich odor of gun oil mingled with high-test exhaust. All these cowboys, armed to the teeth, there was no way he could take them all on. He slumped against a tree, its bark scuffing his cheek. *Fool.* These men had nothing to do with Sandy. He was stupid to think that they'd kidnapped her. She was homeward bound, determined to contact a divorce lawyer as soon as she stepped off the bus.

A stooped, scrawny figure sidled to the edges of the shadows of the porch. The cowboys quieted. Al strained to hear, but he couldn't make out the figure's low, secretive murmur. Al slipped to the nearest tailgate. The speaker's spidery limbs and the perverse, outward foist of his crotch left no doubt. Al sneered. *Billy Bob.* Al squeezed until he could feel the shotgun's stock against his palm. Maybe all he needed to do was to cut off the head of the snake.

Al crept to the corner of the tailgate and grazed along the pickup's side walls, while straining to penetrate the muddle of agitated voices. When he reached the truck's driver-side door, a reedy voice said, "… kidnapping means federal time …"

Al grimaced. So they did have her, they all knew that Billy Bob had her, right there in that cabin, trussed up, gagged. He snarled. The bastards probably meant to gang-rape her.

He raised his head until his eyes were above the truck's nose. Whispers circulated through the crowd. The brims of several cowboy hats nodded. A deeper, tobacco-gruff voice said, "We got a job to do. I say we *getterdone.*"

More hat brims bobbed. Al ducked and stole to the next truck. His careful footfalls seemed to boom in the cowboys' sudden silence, which, he supposed, stressed the traffickers' fealty while Billy Bob, lecturing too low for Al to hear the words, laid down the law. Al squatted and leaned against the truck's quarter panel. He re-gripped the shotgun as the numbness oozed back into his hands. If he rushed them they'd gun him down in two seconds flat. He gnashed his teeth. There must be a way to pull this off.

Behind him, somebody blurted, "Hey!" He twitched and thumped the back of his skull against the truck. As the voice drawled slow, "These orchards are crawling with police," he relocated its source somewhere off to his left. Murmurs rose in agreement.

Al nodded. If he stood up and shouted 'Police, drop your weapons!' he might catch them off guard, and before they knew what was happening, he'd put the gun on Billy Bob, and make the perv take him to Sandy. Once he untied her, she could carry a gun too, and they could take one of the trucks, and they'd drive Billy Bob straight to a police station–

"Hey!"

Al jerked toward the voice. A cowboy, standing at the corner of the truck's grill, was looking straight at him. They stared at each other. Al shot to his feet and shouted, "Police! Drop your weapons! You're under arrest!"

The cowboys scattered. Trucks revved. Fumes burned Al's eyes and intensified a delayed headrush that his sudden motion had induced. He swayed, then blinked his vision clear. Trucks jostled for entry onto the dirt road leading away from the clearing. He zigzagged through the melee toward the cabin.

He bulled through the cabin's three rooms, finding no trace of Sandy. Billy Bob must have secreted her somewhere for his own private, twisted uses. The skeeve, popping Viagra like Tic-Tacs, would ravage her until he got sick of her, then he would sell her into slavery, down south or maybe even in the Middle East.

He rushed to the exit. Trucks logjammed the dirt road. He streaked into the woods and dashed parallel to the dirt road, staying close enough so he could see the trucks through the trees, hoping to catch sight of Billy Bob's big black Ford F150. The trees gave way to a grassy ditch which bordered a road. Trucks roared from the dirt onto the pavement. A stone's throw ahead, another road intersected the paved road. Trucks sped in four directions. He groaned. A massive, shiny black Ford F150 rumbled past him and headed north. He bowed his head and jogged after the truck.

Chapter Fourteen

A pair of darker, blunt shadows skulked into the murky rectangular gap between the threadbare carpet and the bottom of the door. Sandy arched her back into another attempt to rip the eyebolt out of wall behind her, but the steel handcuffs bit into the raw skin of her wrists, and the agony overwhelmed what little strength remained in her deadened muscles. She collapsed back onto the air mattress. Her ass thumped against floorboards before the under-inflated mattress rebounded. Her arms, stretched behind her head, sagged. The shackles joining her ankles clinked.

The shadows under the doorsill shuffled. The goon, working up the nerve barge in and rape her. Or Hennig working up the nerve to murder her. He couldn't let her go, or she'd blow the lid off his little scheme to corporatize the pollination industry. For money, they, *he*, murdered her son. She gazed up into the naked bulb in light fixture above until her vision shrunk to a pinprick. *If anyone's up there, please, just give me one more fair shot at him.*

The door whooshed open. The doorframe forced the goon to angle his Neanderthalish body and to duck his balding head, his haste causing the lank tangles horseshoeing his skull to sway. Lust clouded his tiny eyes. His right iris jittered. His upright erection contoured club-like against his tight jeans.

She stilled herself. His stealth as he eased the door shut behind himself made it obvious that he was sneaking behind Hennig's back. She could scream, but first she'd rather take this chance to make the huge pervert scream.

He plopped down in the corner against the door. He removed his big clodhoppers, then his socks. She averted her nose from the waft of unwashed feet. Her gaze swept over the paper-thin gray carpet to the dirty white wall and up to the shuttered window. The night's darkness rimmed the blinds' slats and edges. From her low position, the slats' downward slant allowed an angled view of the ghostly white blossoms crowding the trailer.

The sandpapery scratch on her other side drew her attention. On hands and knees he crawled toward her. His tongue lolled. His filthy tee-shirt hung from his bony torso. The knees of jeans scuffed the carpet. Barefooted, he clutched his balled up socks in his right hand. He meant to cram those yellowed socks into her mouth.

She had to muster all her willpower not to cry out to Hennig, who, for all she knew, might be sanctioning the goon's taste for rape. Next to her, the goon reared up on his knees. He stabbed the balled up socks at her mouth. She swiveled her face. He crammed the sweaty fabric against her cheek. He wiped a slimy trail across her face in search of her mouth. Disgust kept her wrenching her head back and forth, even as his unexpected patience sapped her efforts. She twisted her body away from him and pressed her face into the mattress. The realization hit her, that he wouldn't be going through the trouble to gag her if Hennig had given him the go-ahead.

She calmed. She reminded herself that she'd already figured out that she could call out if she had to. She put up no resistance as he yanked her back towards him. The goon pressed the stinky mass against her closed lips. The wretched fumes burned her eyes. The stench invaded her nostrils. She swiped her face away from him.

He growled. He palmed her head with his massive left hand. The power in his fingers felt as if he could crush her skull like an eggshell. He lifted his right leg to straddle her. She bit back a smile. She flexed her abs and outstretched arms. She used the eyebolt as an anchor to add snap to her knee lift. Her ankles joined, she let her left knee knock his raised leg wider as she drove her right knee straight into his balls.

He gasped. His rancid breath made her gag. He rolled over her and onto the carpet on the other side of the mattress. He cradled his testicles with his right hand while back-fisting the floor with his left, thump, thump, thump. His mouth gaped. His chest and stomach spasmed.

She snorted her nostrils and spat her mouth clear of his reek.

He flopped over and pressed up to his hands and knees, then with a long groan he reeled to his feet. His erection had shriveled to a modest bulge against the front of his jeans. Rage burned the cloudiness from his eyes. His right iris shook fast enough to blur. His knuckles cracked as his flexed his mallet-like fists. He took a lunging stride toward her, his balled-up socks abandoned on the carpet behind him.

"Francis!"

Hennig stood on the threshold, glowering, his left hand on his hip, his right index finger pointed at the goon, who stopped dead in his tracks. Hennig stepped out of the doorway and into the room, while shifting his index finger away from the goon and towards the vacated exit. "Go!"

The goon stepped over her. His head hung so low she caught a glimpse of his red cheeks. Hennig closed the door behind him. Hennig softened his stern expression while looking down on her. "I apologize. Business forced me to leave him alone with you. I'll try to keep a more vigilant watch on him from here on out."

She glared at *him*. Hell would freeze over before …

He bent down and seized her hips. She tensed. Hot tears threatened to slip from her eyes. The possibility that she might cry in front of him and her abject helplessness further fueled her outrage.

"Relax," he murmured. "I have no such urges."

He slid her upward, relieving some of the stress on her arms. "There." He straightened and took a backward step. "Of course, you must have realized by now that Francis is challenged. He is going through a delayed adolescence, and strong hormones have wilded him a bit."

She sniffled as quietly as she could. The intense green of his small eyes sparkled. She suspected that not much escaped his notice. She seethed to accuse him, but she couldn't unclench her jaw, couldn't unclamp her teeth. The temperature in her head soared, increasing the strain to keep from bawling in front of him.

Hennig's smooth, practiced tone infuriated her so much so that she saw double images of him, as he said, "Francis informed me about your suicidal attempt at sabotage."

She managed to part her teeth and to get her tongue moving. "You murdered my son."

He bowed his head. The single bulb's harsh light flashed off the bare spots where pale skin showed through the patches of stunted red hairs, the pathetic results of hair-growth chemicals. *Now comes his 'heartfelt' apology.* "I'm very sorry for what happened to your son. It was a terrible, terrible accident."

She bit her tongue till she tasted blood. The bastard refused to take direct responsibility for Mikey's death.

He skirted her and stepped up to the window. He gazed outside, his hands clasped behind his back. *So he doesn't have to look me in the eye.* He mused, "Far too late to back out now."

His loose blue polo shirt and tan slacks hung from his slight frame. He looked like a child playing dress-up in his father's clothes. She refused to take the bait, knowing that he was trying to prompt her into asking questions, trying to draw her into a conversation, trying to make himself seem human. He only wanted her to accept his apology in order to avoid the legal repercussions. He probably staged the goon's attempted rape so he could ride in on his white horse and save her. Well, he didn't have to worry about jail or lawsuits. All she wanted was to get her hands around his scrawny neck.

"I want you to understand that we're going to great lengths for your sake."

She exerted measured tension against the eyebolt. She increased the pull but felt no give. She reached the limits of her reserves and released as quietly as she could. She couldn't stop imagining the sequence of ripping the bolt out of the wall and falling on the bastard, then ramming the bolt's sharp end into his eye socket as he screamed for mercy until it pierced his brain.

He pivoted and made eye contact with her. "What I'm trying to impress on you is that you are making our task much more difficult."

She hissed, "So murder me, like you murdered my son!"

He assumed a sad expression, obviously faking it, and said, "You know who I am, I've shown myself to you. The fact that you are not dead, your corpse lying in a shallow grave, should prove to you that I do not mean you any harm. But in the meantime, I cannot allow you to be a disruption."

She coughed up a bitter laugh. "You think your corporate masters will let you free me? You think they haven't murdered people before? You think it's not obvious that the same bees that killed Mikey stung Sven?"

He tilted his head, raised an eyebrow in acknowledgement.

"Once you've planted evidence that discredits beekeepers, makes them look like the cause of CCD, you think your masters are gonna let me go?"

A little smile played on his thin pale lips. "You've figured it all out then?"

"I've had some time to think things through." She bit back a wince, wishing she hadn't even conversed that much. "You're planting infected bees in independent beekeepers' hives. They spread the disease. You sic your killer bees on people, to make it look like the independents can't control their bees, like they're rank amateurs, and then they're wide open to attacks, so you can accuse them of overuse, mismanagement, whatever, and the charges will stick. They get blamed for CCD, and at the same time, their hives are ruined, and they go out of business. Then your corporate masters step in and take complete control over the industry, and then there's nobody at all to make any noise about CCD, and the whole thing goes away. You basically said so at the convention."

His smiled widened. The skin at the corner of his eyes creased. "You have an interesting mind."

She bared her teeth. "You murdered my son, for money!"

His smile dried up. "Do you really believe that my employers, for such a delicate and subtle act of corporate espionage, would send me and my Mongoloid nephew to carry out their wicked plans?"

Her chest deflated. She hadn't thought of that, but she'd be damned before she said so to him.

He strode to the door. "There's a lot more at stake than you realize. I'm examining every angle, trying to construct a scenario wherein you survive. But so far, I find it difficult to believe that you will forgive my tragic mistake and allow both for your survival and the plan's success." He placed his index finger on the light switch. "Now, try to get some rest. You have a long day ahead of you tomorrow."

He flicked off the light and left, shutting the door behind him. In the darkness, the hours dribbled away while pieces of different theories whirled around her mind, but she couldn't make anything fit into a coherent scenario before exhaustion finally dragged her down to unconsciousness.

Chapter Fifteen

An unbroken bloody red overflowed Al's vista. Instinct impelled him to open his eyes, but the lids, gummed together, resisted, the skin stretching, until the seal broke with a slight pop. Sunlight seared into his eyeballs, and sharpened and recentered the dull throb in his temples to a migraine screeching against interior bone behind his brow.

He scrunched his eyes shut. He flailed for soothing blackness but he couldn't escape the raging red. He rubbed his eyelids, eased them open, let in the light by degrees. The world blurred. He tried to blink up some moisture but objects remained smears of color against a wavy background, and only those images warping double achieved anything like coherency.

A dizzy spell forced him to close his eyes and to lay his head back into the hot grass. He gagged, his ribs heaving, his throat raw, so he turned his lips to the side, but nothing came up. The skin inside his mouth seemed to crack, and his desert-dry tongue suppressed his voice as he tried to mumble, "Oh god …"

He clenched his fists, crushing silky petals. *Almond trees. Fucking almond trees.* He capsized over to his belly. One handhold at a time he dragged his battered body until coolness enveloped upon him, and shady darkness descended over the red scorching his eyelids.

He slackened. He breathed, one cheek pressed into the soft pillow of petals and grass. Only his grumbling belly and parched throat kept his deep breaths from becoming snores.

He raised his head. He cracked his eyelids. His vision shimmered, then a trailer coalesced. He squinted. *No way.* His trailer. His hives, *their* hives. He shook his head, but the sight persisted. He flopped back down to the ground and cackled. He decided to rest just a little bit more, then he'd crawl over and get himself a glass of water, and make himself a peanut butter and jelly sandwich with the crusts cut off … he winced, and lurched around and clawed at the almond tree's bark until he winched himself up to his feet.

His leaden hamstrings refused to straighten. He groaned. He placed one palm against the tree and let his head droop. His knees and ankles throbbed. *Why?* Snatches of the previous night's mission dribbled back to him. Following Billy Bob's big black truck, on foot. Crashing through the orchards, skidding across gravel roads, at least once tumbling ass over heels, not seeing a ditch in the pitch darkness. He must have jogged half the night away.

He whispered, "Idiot." The trickle of memories increased to a flood. He screwed his eyes shut and blocked out his folly. He didn't want to know why his elbows, his shoulder joints, hell, even his fingers, ached. He was gonna hobble to the trailer, grab the nearest phone, and call the goddamned police. Unless, of course, Sandy was sitting in the living room, arms folded over her chest, one leg crossed over the other at the knee, the top leg performing fast, pissed-off half-kicks …

A piercing, hypodermic needle-like pain plunged into his forearm. He hissed. A giant bee had its electric yellow and black ringed abdomen pressed against his flesh, its stinger buried deep. On reflex he smacked the bee, the blow rebounding off its tough exoskeleton. A flurry of frantic smacks squashed the bee. Its guts oozed around the jagged black stinger and drizzled to the ground. The mottled and lumpy condition of his skin startled him. A numbness swirled around the fresh sting, then spread down to his fingers and up his arm. His eyes rolled up into his head. He moaned as he slumped to his knees, then to his back. The rush scrolled up his brain, accelerating to supersonic speeds, obliterating his consciousness. Technicolor explosions crackled against a sizzling black and white backdrop, the sizzling growing into white noise, which cranked louder and louder until he thought his eardrums would burst.

The bottom dropped out, out of the noise, out of his stomach, and the din evaporated into silence as he floated downward, to and fro, like a feather dropped from a jet, the jaw-dropping distance terrifying, but the lazy pace, and the fluffy quiet swaddling him, drawing him back from the brown-acid abyss.

A bang snapped him out of his stupor. He raised his head. He gazed past the toes of his boots and muttered, "What the …"

An alien … no, an astronaut … no, some freaky-tall dude wearing the weirdest beekeeping suit he'd ever seen, bounded down the trailer's steps. The suit's space-age, pristine white and the bizarre cylindrical helmet made Al think of Hazmat suits. A bit of powder pink dangled from the gangly freak's gloved fist. *Sandy's panties*? The beekeeper stuffed the pink prize into a small duffel bag atop one of the hive bodies.

The beekeeper stooped to a beer cooler-sized container next to the hives. He opened the lid of the smooth white container.

Al whispered, "What the fuck are you doing to my bees?" He slunk around the almond tree. He spied on the beekeeper, who pulled a tray halfway out of the hive, then shifted so that the white expanse of his back blocked Al's view.

I knew it.

Al smiled, exposing clamped teeth. They'd isolated the virus, and reverse-engineered the cause of CCD. The clandestine beekeeper was most likely injecting a hotshot cocktail of pesticides, herbicides, and chemical accelerants into his hives. His smile twisted into a sneer. They meant to frame him.

From the container the beekeeper removed a tray nearly as thin as a sheet of paper. The beekeeper slid the tray into the hive body. Al frowned, then his brow smoothed as he exhaled, "Ahhhh." Of course Billy Bob was in bed with the pesticide companies. Made sense. His cover as *the* high and mighty honeybee broker depended on the pollination industry. Of course he would have dealings with the big muckity-mucks of the pesticide industry. Probably CIA connected up the ass throughout all the corporate bigwigs. All Billy Bob had to do was pick up the phone and call somebody, say something like, 'It looks like we have a mutual problem. Can you take care of it?'

Al nodded. So they set him up, make him look like the typhoid Mary of CCD. Probably at this very moment, they were messing with the hives back at the farm, planting evidence that would destroy him.

He tilted forward, then caught himself preparing to blitz the beekeeper. He rasped, "Whoa, boy, simmer down." The beekeeper would be armed. Al had a vague recollection of toting a shotgun. He scanned the grounds. No gun, but his eyes zeroed in on the strange pickup, blue, shiny new, and his next move dawned on him. *Be patient.*

The beekeeper closed the container's lid and worked its latch. He zipped up his little bag and slung it over his shoulder. Al glared. Sandy's time was running out. The panty raid proved that her captors were perverts. Who knew what those sick bastards were planning to do to her. Al shifted his weight from foot to foot. There was no time to call the cops, who were probably in Billy Bob's pockets anyways.

Al fidgeted while the beekeeper loaded the container into the fancy blue truck's bed. Once the beekeeper got in the cab and started the engine, Al launched into a ducking dash. As the truck rolled, he grabbed the tailgate and slipped over the top into the bed. He wormed right up to the back of the cab and curled into the fetal position. He expected a sudden stop, and the beekeeper's shout, but the truck kept accelerating. He glanced down his arms, and casually flicked away the half dozen or so bees stinging him. He grinned. The perv would drive him straight to Sandy.

Chapter Sixteen

The truck jolted to a stop. Its engine rumbled. Al clutched the wrench he'd scrounged among the bric-a-brac in the truck's bed. He still hadn't settled on whether to jump the driver or to hide. He peeked over the bed's wall. A rundown white trailer clogged the wide spot in the service road's dirt slash through the orchard's endless pinkish-white. Definitely not Billy Bob's headquarters.

Al angled his head, rolled his eyes upwards, and through the cab's rear window, caught a glimpse on the driver's balding head. The driver held a cell phone to his ear. *Now or never*. Al kept his eyes on the driver as he slunk over the wall on the passenger's side. He hit the dirt and, on his back, scrabbled under the truck.

He re-gripped the wrench one finger at a time. The engine died. The truck's door squealed open. The big white boots, the only items of the weird beekeeping outfit that the driver hadn't shucked, thumped to the dirt. Al's forehead bumped the truck's undercarriage as he watched the boots clomp over to the tailgate.

The driver unloaded the dolly, then stacked the weird ceramic containers on the dolly's blade. Al tensed. Maybe the driver was getting the important stuff out of harm's way before he pounced. Maybe this remote trailer, one of the dozens Billy Bob rented out, or rather, deducted the expense from the fees he paid beekeepers, served as a hideout. Maybe Billy Bob and his stooges were lurking in there right now plotting the best way to deal with him. Al supposed their assault wouldn't take long since he'd pretty much gift-wrapped himself for the bastards.

The driver banged the tailgate shut into its latches, then trundled the dolly towards a pre-fab aluminum shed next to the trailer. Maybe the driver hadn't noticed him … or maybe not until the goon noticed the wrench was missing. The driver unlocked the shed and wheeled the dolly into the darkness.

Al shifted his head to the opposite side. Maybe he'd better make a break for it before they came after him in numbers. He squeezed the wrench. They'd have guns. He shifted his head back the other way. He frowned. The trailer, the truck, the shed, a vehicle that looked like a golf cart, but no hives. No hives, during the Chase, in this era of CCD and the slow death of independent beekeeping, with Billy Bob waving six figure checks at everybody with the means to come pollinate the Valley? No, this was part of some plan, something set up a while ago, probably well before he and Sandy even set out on this trip. They didn't have Sandy. She was halfway home by now. He grimaced. She was making appointments with divorce attorneys, she was not the prisoner of some white slavery ring.

A screen-door rattle startled Al. His angle allowed him a view of the approacher's brown work boots and faded jeans up to the knees. The boots, way smaller than the driver's, charted a beeline for Al's position. Maybe the boots' owner meant to get in the truck and drive away. Al glanced toward his toes. He wasn't sure the undercarriage would clear his body. He tried to swallow the dry wad in the back of his throat.

The shoes stopped a few feet away from the truck's rear tire. Al held his breath. He willed his body towards absolute stillness, absolute silence.

"Come on out, Mister Rhodes."

Al snapped rigid. *It can't be.*

"Please, Mister Rhodes."

Al struggled to catch his breath. Faint, swirling white noise gathered deep in his brain.

"I have a gun, Mister Rhodes, but my fondest wish is that I shall not need it."

Al shook his head 'No.' The impulse to see for sure what his ears testified to as the god's honest truth drove him to shimmy toward that smug, oily voice, which he'd heard so often on the Web and in person that one damned time … He poked his head out from under the truck. "You!"

Hennig raised his red eyebrows, the motion crinkling his otherwise smooth pale forehead. Behind his black frame glasses, His small green eyes widened. He trained a handgun on Al. "They sent *you* to kill me?"

Al stopped, lying halfway out from under the truck. He scrutinized Hennig's face, the small mouth, the few freckles smattering the bridge of his nose, but he saw no lie in the man's steady gaze.

Hennig tilted his face back and clucked his tongue. "So that's why you interrupted my presentation. They were already on to me.

They knew what I was about to say, so they planted you in the audience." He lowered his head and glared at Al from under his eyebrows. He growled, "Come out of there. Now!"

Al clambered out and rose. He stood a couple inches or so above Hennig. He swayed, scrunched his eyes against the headrush, then, as the roaring decayed, he opened his eyes and focused on Hennig.

Hennig's eyes widened further. "My god look what they've done to you. I-I-I can't believe you're still alive!"

Al teetered, regained his balance, did a slow, hard blink, then managed to slur, "Huh?"

"The stings! My associate and I have taken every precaution to avoid even a single sting, but you, you must have sustained dozens!"

Al opened his mouth, but he couldn't process a response to Hennig's use of the word 'They.'

Hennig's face darkened. "So, that's how you meant to do it. Screwed up somehow, though." He nodded. "They must have given you some kind of serum, just in case the killer bees got out and got you before you could set them on me."

"What?"

"Don't play dumb. It doesn't suit you, Mister Rhodes. I knew it was only a matter of time before they discovered I was amassing evidence against them, before they discovered that I was working against them from the inside. But I never dreamed that you were working for them, that you were one of them."

A spasm shot through Al's head. He blurted, "No!"

"Very impassioned. I can see why they chose you. But perhaps you'd like to explain what you were doing hiding under the truck, or why you followed my associate."

Al toot a half-step back, his backside touching the truck. "I caught your *associate* tampering with my hives!"

Hennig snorted. "My associate was gathering evidence, and attempting to exterminate the killer bees, killer bees housed in *your* hives."

Al shook his head while mouthing the word, 'No.'

"I understand that a killer bee stung your employee. The bee must have escaped en route."

Al exhaled through his nostrils. He was being framed. They were framing him.

Hennig's eyelids dropped to slits. "What I cannot understand, what I simply cannot comprehend, is why you continue to serve them after they caused your tragic loss ..."

Searing pain erupted deep in his guts. A quaking burr increased to jackhammer velocity, shaking his field of vision until the world smeared all tracers and blurs. He emitted a strangled, wavering whine, then he clamped his teeth and eyes shut so hard that his jaw popped. The shaking withdrew, receding back down his head, down his chest, draining into his guts, which finally quieted. He opened his eyes to see the gun pointed straight at his face.

Hennig looked Al up and down, then said, "On the other hand, you don't appear to be armed."

Al hissed, "I'm not."

"But I cannot imagine any other explanation for why you were skulking beneath my associate's truck ... unless, hmmm."

Al was about to tell all about Billy Bob and Sandy, but Hennig said, "Perhaps you happened upon my associate, and perplexed, you stowed away in the truck, seeking answers as to why this stranger was tampering with your hives."

"Yes! Billy Bob, he's got Sandy!"

Hennig twitched backward, then said, "I see."

Al leaped into Hennig's hesitation. "Billy Bob ... CIA drug smuggling! Human trafficking!"

Henning, in a slow cadence, said, "So Billy Bob uses his position as the region's top honeybee broker as a cover for drug smuggling and human trafficking. He's a CIA asset, so they run interference for him. At the same time, given the CIA's obvious swinging door policy with corporate America, when the agricultural-industrial complex desires some kind of black operation in this sector, they turn to Billy Bob."

"Yes!"

Hennig nodded. "That makes all the sense in the world. And you somehow discovered Billy Bob's involvement, so now he means to silence you. Naturally you assumed that my associate was one of Billy Bob's henchmen, planting evidence to frame you."

"Yes!"

"They took advantage of our animosity, which, I remind you, was feigned on my part, as I was simply playing a part, pretending to be their puppet, their mouthpiece, while I gathered information. Pitting us against one another … a stroke of genius. Should the two of us be found dead at each other's hands, Billy Bob wouldn't have to lift a finger!"

Al staggered, then said, "What?"

Hennig lowered the gun to his side. He looked Al in the eyes. "We have to figure out how to best use this turn of events." He gave his head a slight swivel to the left and peered at Al. "Does he know that you're on to him?"

Al nodded.

"But he doesn't know that I know, or that we've discovered a common cause." He snapped his fingers. "I got it! Here." He handed Al the gun. "I'll be right back."

Al stared at the gun in his hand. He scoffed. He looked up in time to see Hennig spring up the steps and into the trailer. He muttered, "No way." He checked the clip, sure that it'd be empty, but he found it full, with a round jacked into the chamber. *Working against them from the inside.*

He slipped his index finger into the trigger guard. He strode towards the trailer. A mini-headrush geysered. He stopped. Billy Bob, the CIA, drug smuggling, human trafficking, murder, the black market sex industry … Al winced. He couldn't fit Doctor Dean Hennig into that picture.

He stared at the trailer while his vision stabilized. Hennig was an academic. They wouldn't have sent the doctor and his associate out here to do a frame job. They would have sent a team of black-ops specialists. Occupying an unused trailer, Hennig, and probably a faithful lab assistant, working fast and loose, that fit the picture. Hennig, after years of living high on the hog while propagating the industry's lies, caught wind of what they meant to do to Al, and finally their evil became too great to swallow, and he decided to do something about it. That fit.

Al, surprised to find himself aiming the gun at the trailer, let his arm fall to his side.

Hennig reappeared, hurrying down the steps and carrying a blue backpack. He strode towards Al. Henning gave him the pack.

"There's water and nutrition bars, extra ammunition, and a change of clothes."

Al shouldered the pack.

Hennig turned sideways. "I'd give you the keys to the truck, but you've got a better chance of getting close without them knowing if you go on foot." He gestured a little south of the sun. "That way, straight to his headquarters."

Hennig locked eyes with Al. "Take up a position within sight of his compound. My associate and I have some loose ends to tie up here, and then the whole world will know what my erstwhile masters have been up to. Then we'll come, create a diversion, and you go in and get your wife."

Al stammered, then said, "I don't know what to say."

Hennig offered his hand. While Al clasped his hand, Hennig said, "Good luck. I'll see you on the other side."

Al set his jaw, then bounced into a jog, heading into the orchard in the direction Hennig indicated.

Chapter Seventeen

Sandy perched on the edge of the sprung couch that bordered the back wall of the trailer's tiny living room. Hennig's voice, his words indistinguishable, carried through the trailer's thin outer walls. Across the room, Francis slouched, peeking around the edges of the side window's blinds.

She rubbed her thumb over the ribs of the plastic casing of the box cutter that she hid in her fist. Again, she performed the calculations, visualized herself crossing the short span of brown carpet between them before he could react. Usually, when Hennig wasn't watching, Francis ogled her breasts while openly playing with himself. She grimaced. This might be her best chance.

She stared at his white boots, incongruous with his jeans and sallow tee-shirt. His BO wafted across the room and made her wrinkle her nose. He inched the blinds' edge over and let a slant of sunlight into the darkened living room. She'd been lugging one of those ceramic containers, her sweaty hands slipping on the container's smooth surface, when Hennig got the call. They'd hurried back here, in such a rush that he forgot to confiscate the box cutter that he'd lent her for her morning chores. When Francis arrived at the trailer, Hennig had gone out, come back in to fetch a backpack, then gone out again. Some crisis that demanded the good doctor's attention. Maybe the cops. She considered screaming her lungs out, but Hennig might be conferring with another henchman, and she would surely lose the few privileges her meekness had won.

She glanced at the door, then back to the filthy carpet between her feet. She could just make a break for it. She'd scrutinized Francis, but his clothing showed no telltale bulges of a hidden gun. Still, she didn't move. Most guys didn't have much of a size advantage on her, but Francis sure did.

Hennig's dampened voice fell silent. Francis whirled around and took a long stride towards her. Lust glassed his eyes. She surged off the couch. She pressed the box cutter's catch, but angled it wrong, and the blade stuck inside the casing. She slowed her arcing swing as she worked at the catch. Francis got his arm up. The jarring impact of his bony arm almost smacked the box cutter from her hand. He seized her other arm and spun her into a downward semicircle. He bulldogged her onto her belly. His body crashed on top of her, knocking the wind out of her. She tried to scratch out from under him, but he held her down. His overwhelming strength forced a frustrated growl from her lips.

He lifted his torso a bit. The panting of his rotten-egg breath buffeted her ear. He flipped her onto her back. He used one knee to pin her legs and the other to guard his crotch. His eyes fixated on her breasts. Drool drizzled from his open mouth onto her cheek. He released one of her arms and pawed at the neck of her tee shirt. His fingers hooked into the flimsy material. He stretched the shirt toward him. She pressed the box cutter's catch. She thumbed the blade out of its casing. She thrust her fist around the tented material of her tee shirt, then whipped the blade back towards herself, across his neck.

Hot blood spattered over her breastbone. He clutched his neck and pitched off of her. Hacking, she lunged for the couch. She used the thin cushions to push herself to her feet. She raked the hair out of her eyes and lowered into a crouch, ready to use the razor blade again. He curled into the fetal position with his back to her, and with both hands gripping his throat. He let out a low gurgle.

Hennig filled the doorway. She took a step back into the far corner. She brandished the bloodied cutter at him. Hennig had no size advantage on her. She coiled, preparing to blitz him.

Hennig pulled a handgun out of the back of his waistband. He leveled the gun at her. "Don't do it."

She teetered on the edge of leaping, then settled back onto her heels.

"Drop it," he said.

She tossed the box cutter, which thumped against the carpet between them.

He kept the gun trained on her as he stepped over to Francis, who had stilled. he stooped, checked his pulse, then straightened. "He's dead."

"He attacked me. He tried to rape me." *Stupid*! She should've never dropped the box cutter. He was gonna kill her anyways. She glimpsed its green case against the brown at the bottom of her peripheral vision. She figured the chances of getting to it and getting to him before he could pull the trigger fell somewhere between slim to none. But he might miss.

Hennig sighed. He pushed his black-frame glasses back up his nose. "It's my fault. I knew his hormones were getting the better of him. I should have never left him alone with you. I apologize."

Sandy froze. She caught herself gaping, and she closed her mouth.

Hennig regarded Francis. "Perhaps it's for the best. His limitations were a great hindrance, but, his behavioral issues, well, I don't have to tell you that he was spiraling out of control, in spite of the best care money could buy."

Hennig looked up at her. "Now, your assistance is crucial. Now, you'll be with me until the end."

"Until the end of what?"

"You've got blood on you. Go wash it off. Change your clothes, then get the shower curtain. We'll need to dig a grave."

Sandy glanced at the bloody box cutter. She pivoted and headed down the narrow hallway towards the bathroom. Hennig didn't show much of an emotional response to his nephew's death. *Sociopath.* She bit her lip. But what about her own lack of response? She searched herself. She couldn't find a scrap of remorse for the would-be rapist, mentally-challenged or not. Maybe she was in shock.

She eased the ruined shirt over her head, careful to keep the blood-soaked portions away from her face. Now that there was only one of them, it should be a helluva lot easier to escape. But without Francis, he needed her, all the way to the end, he said. She knew from her studies that people like him would never trust anybody. But maybe she could get him to drop his guard far enough so that she could learn exactly what his plans were.

She wadded up the shirt as she turned into the bathroom. She would be a good girl. If she did escape, she might not make it to the authorities in time to stop him from doing whatever he was doing.

Chapter Eighteen

Sandy barely felt the green dolly's rounded grip through the thick material of the oversized white gloves. Even though they'd only gone a few paces from the cart, her arms trembled, and her aching back thrummed. Digging Francis' shallow grave had wiped her out.

She ground her teeth, but Francis' rotten breath lingered in the helmet and thwarted her attempt to force him out of her thoughts. Socks filled the toes of his former boots, reminding her of that rancid sock he shoved into her mouth the first time he tried to rape her. Not once, but twice he tried to rape her. She snarled. She forced the fact that she murdered a mentally-challenged man deep down into her guts, where the guilt simmered, then threatened to froth upwards. She ground her teeth harder. Hennig was responsible, just like he was responsible for the death of her son.

She glanced at Hennig, who also suited up, head to toe, against the danger of the bees. She couldn't see his eyes through his helmet's black visor. She wondered if the sadness they showed during Francis' burial persisted. For the first time, she wondered if Mikey's death weighed on him.

The glimmer of sympathy for the murderer made her wince. In order to head off a fresh wave of shame, she said, "I don't understand what we're doing. What with the CCD scare, the beekeepers will be checking their hives all the time. Won't they realize their queens are gone?"

Through his helmet his voice sounded hushed and distant as he said, "I grew up poor."

She frowned. The white suit disguised his body language, but his shoulders seemed slumped, and his head bowed.

"Used to be a race between me and my siblings on grocery day," he said, "to see who could gobble down the good stuff the fastest, so the others didn't get it." He let out a single dry laugh. "Then it was another two weeks or so of peanut butter sandwiches and macaroni and cheese before the next grocery day."

She kept her smile small, even though she knew he couldn't see it. She went through pretty much the same thing with Alice, Danny, and Ben. She was pretty sure those early battles for food sparked the resentments they all still cherished against one another, the resentments that surfaced, like clockwork, every Thanksgiving and Christmas.

"My father ran off when I was very young," he said. "His absence put a lot of pressure on my mother. She was forced to resort to welfare and food stamps. Really, it is only lately that I am able to fully appreciate the pressure she was under. It astounds me that she was able to hold it together."

Sandy sniffed. She was only three when her own father drowned in a flood. Her mother went to work at a factory. Sandy was never quite sure what they made there, but she knew that no matter how hard her mother scrubbed, she always had a little black grime rimming her fingernails. Sandy also never knew how much they paid her mother, but she remembered long stretches when they couldn't afford the phone, and one time the power company shut the electricity off for a week. Cancer took her mother about a year after she finally got Danny out of the house.

"My first job was a paper route," Hennig said, "when I was eleven. I never stopped working, worked all the way through college."

"So if you know what it's like to be poor, why do you work for them?"

"What are your feelings about climate change?"

She glowered at him until she remembered he couldn't see her face. "I think it's common sense."

"Go on."

"It drives me up the wall, that the same people that claim common sense whenever it suits them, on a whole range of issues, all of a sudden have none when it comes to stuff like pollution."

"You put dirt in a glass of water, you get dirty water."

"Yes!" She caught herself, dialed back her enthusiasm to a calm tone. "Exactly."

"You pump billions upon billions of tons of pollutants into the environment, you will cause … *unpleasant* changes. It's common sense, even if the overwhelming scientific opinion wasn't confirming that simple commonsense conclusion. And those scientists on the other side, they are either in the employ of the worst polluters, and so merely spreading corporate propaganda, or, perhaps a few are hacks desperate to differentiate themselves in some way, seeking to make a name for themselves by being controversial."

She let go of the dolly's grip with her left hand and shook an impending cramp out of her forearm, the motion causing her baggy suit to rustle. She resituated her left hand on the grip before the dolly swerved. "But ..."

"But I'm one of those corporate propagandists."

"Yeah. But you believe in climate change?"

"Of course *global warming* is real, not to mention a looming catastrophe."

She huffed. She sputtered, then managed to say, "Then why?" The silence stretched between them until she couldn't take it anymore. "The money?"

"I won't deny that the money is, well, superlative. But the money is not why I do what I do. Have you ever argued with somebody who denies the facts of global warming?"

She nodded. Not even a year ago, in Ethics, when the class moved to environmental issues, a small pocket of flat-Earthers refused to budge no matter what. Sometimes, the nights after that class met, her frustration and anger at their refusal to accept the facts kept her lying awake for hours in the dark. "Yes."

"So you understand that such efforts are complete wastes of energy."

"I do now."

"I saw only one way to get into the room, let alone a seat at the table."

She stopped and sized him up. "You mean to tell me that you were pretending all this time?"

He shrugged. "I'm not so arrogant that I believed I could just walk in and overwhelm them with the force of my personality. But I know what I'm good at. I'm good at chipping away at huge tasks. It's what made me successful in college." He waved to resume movement.

She grunted while getting the dolly rolling again. "But all those people watching you on TV and listening on radio ..."

"Preaching to the choir. I doubt I persuaded many people. The deniers just want to hear somebody saying what they already believe. When I first charted this course, after surveying the situation thoroughly, it was the lethargy on our side that most dismayed me."

"Huh." She knew what he was talking about. She saw it among her fellow college students, the kids who should've been up in arms. It was their future, after all, that was being ruined at a breakneck pace, but they were too busy with their smartphones and keggers, not to mention their class loads, to work up enough energy for this critical issue.

"The more outrageous claims I could dream up, the angrier I made the opposition, the more I energized them, and, even more crucial, the more I politicized previous non-political people. I made myself into an effigy of all that is wrong with the right wing, so that lefties could rally themselves against me. I must say, it worked far better than I envisioned."

She snorted. Al would stay up half the night, tapping away on the keyboard, posting manifestos and screeds against big Ag, and against Hennig himself. She wondered how many others Hennig had inspired to such passion.

"At the same time, I've been able to slightly influence my various employers, although that is a much more delicate project. The best arguments I could make are from an economic standpoint, which would seem out of my wheelhouse, and thus throw suspicion on me. Most often, the best I can do is to make it clear, either explicitly, or implicitly, that we are engaged in persuading the public away from the truth, and so work on the consciences of those who make the big decisions."

"So is that what we're doing? Are we doing something that's going to make the power brokers think twice?"

"Here's good."

She pulled the dolly up next to a jumble of hive bodies, the wooden cases splintery, their white paintjob peeling.

"We're behind schedule," he said. "It'll be more efficient if we split up. You know what to do. You finish up here, I'll come back around and pick you up."

Her chin touched the bottom edge on the interior of her helmet as he strode back to the cart, then hopped in and puttered away, disappearing into the orchard's dense pinkish white. When she could no longer hear the whine of the cart's motor, she pivoted towards the dirty white trailer. There must be a phone somewhere inside.

She took a single step. *A test.* He would sneak back, or, whoever he was talking to outside the trailer this morning was spying on her. She scanned the trailer's dark windows. Maybe the mystery man was lurking inside, ready to murder her if she tried to escape.

She bent down and touched her toes, hoping to make her step away from the dolly look like she wanted room to stretch her achy muscles. The stretch did feel good, and she added a little volume to her moan, and she held the pose, buying time to think. Her chest constricted as the image of Francis, curled up in the fetal position, his blood staining the brown carpet, superimposed over the petal-strewn grass.

She scrunched her eyelids shut in order to banish the image. Hennig hadn't blamed her at all for killing Francis, instead shifting the entire responsibility on himself. She exhaled and focused on re-loosening her muscles. He might just be stringing her along so she would do the hard labor, meaning to kill her when he didn't need her anymore.

She straightened up and shook out her arms. Obviously he was not performing some secret operation for his corporate masters, or he'd have better facilities, better equipment, and most of all, better trained subordinates. No, he was up to something that the powers-that-be did not know about. Maybe this was her chance to get him to trust her. If she passed this test, maybe he'd confide in her.

She stared at the dolly and its load of two ceramic containers, and on top of them the little white duffel bag containing the necessary tools. Maybe he really was a good man fighting the good fight. If what he said was true, then he'd basically sacrificed his reputation, not to mention himself, for a cause he believed in, something she never even came close to doing.

She squeezed the dolly's rounded grip. If he was truly a crusader against corporate injustice, then she'd help him. If he was up to something more on the malignant side, she had to get him to trust her in order to find out what he was up to, so she could stop him. She unzipped the bag. She wanted to be finished and ready to go by the time he returned.

Chapter Nineteen

Al stopped at the edge of a clearing in the orchard. He
mopped sweat from his brow. The pinkish-white snow-blindness
receded from his vision. A long, narrow log cabin occupied the
clearing. He recalled the heads of bucks, of bears, and even the head
of a gray wolf adorning the dark paneled walls of the main room,
and sitting at the long unfinished oak table, twenty-odd beekeepers
nursing beers, arguing. *Billy Bob's cabin.*

He un-shouldered the backpack and stooped, placing it on the
petal-strewn ground behind an almond tree. He snorted. Hennig told
him the truth. The dizzies sizzled through his awareness when he
stood up too fast. He placed a palm against the tree's bark in order to
steady himself. He couldn't believe how badly he'd misjudged
Hennig. He rubbed his eyelids. He'd think it over later.

The spell passed. He took a long pull from the canteen, then
double-checked the gun. *Locked and loaded.* He scanned the
vehicles, mostly pickups, lining the dirt road curving back into the
almond orchard. He took a sip from the canteen to wet his dry
mouth. Instead of bickering beekeepers, cold-blooded killers must be
sitting around Billy Bob's table, oiling and loading their guns as the
kingpin outlined his strategy to flush Al out of the orchards and
silence him once and for all. Al slipped behind the tree. Hennig said
he'd create a diversion, but this was a suicide mission.

Al looked to the west. Wouldn't be long before the sun began
to sink beneath the mountain range. He should rest up, eat more
nutrition bars, regain his strength. He sagged against the tree. He
closed his eyes, crinkling the crust of dirt and dried sweat around the
sockets. Far away, but approaching, a bass motif of pain throbbed
from … all over.

A burst of voices caused him to rock back on his heels. Men
exited the cabin. They carried guns. Most toted rifles, shotguns.
Most wore trucker hats, long-sleeved flannel shirts, faded jeans, and
either cowboy or work boots. Mostly middle-aged, white faces. Al
bit his lower lip. He would've expected younger men, at least few
more Latinos, thugs on loan from the cartels …

Al scowled. He focused on a short, plump man, his round
face … Henry Kadaski. Al murmured, "What?" A few faces down, a

great tangled brown Grizzly Adams beard that belonged to Mark Sampson, and next to him, Timmy Mosca, Al would know that beanpole anywhere. All three men were beekeepers.

Al dropped his gun hand to his hip. Either they were in on it, or … a beekeeper meeting. A series of tremors quaked through his frame. He bowed his head. *What am I doing?* These men were his peers. He ought to break cover and run to them. They'd know if Sandy had taken off. Surely, by now, if she was safe and on a bus headed home, the rumors would've circulated throughout their little community. He could suck it up and endure the shame to know for sure. And if they didn't know, then they sure as hell could help look for her. He took a deep breath, inflating his chest to the max, and raised his head.

A high-crowned tan cowboy hat crested a tight cluster of men. A turquoise Brahma bull cinched the hat's band. A silver diamond pattern decorated the black band. Al knew that hat. The men parted, revealing the longish white hair sticking out of the back of that hat and draping over the man's collar. The white sideburns and bushy white handlebar mustache left no doubt.

Billy Bob craned out of his stoop until he stood ramrod straight, his big crooked nose a little up in the air, his rigid posture the spitting image of Al's old man. Al slumped, resting his forehead against the tree's rough bark. He stared at the toes of his dirty, scuffed boots. With his left hand he scratched his right forearm. His old man's stony tone echoed in his head, bawling Al out for running all over tarnation like a wild man. His old man's regret, for bringing such a disappointment into the world, needled Al, as the father loomed over his cowed son, who sat at the kitchen table, taking great pains to not put his elbows on the tabletop's unmarred finish. Al's eyes zeroed in on the dark whorls underneath the coat of varnish as the old man berated him for dousing Kenny Camplain's backyard with gasoline and lighting the grass on fire, and for Principal Hart catching him and Conkey smoking behind the concession stand at the middle school and getting a week's in-school suspension, and for a bunch of them partying and crashing George Plemmons' Econoline into the ditch after winning the regional pennant, and … Al exhaled through his nose, his eyelids lowering to slits, while recalling the night he told his old man that Sandy was pregnant and he was gonna marry her, and his old man insisting that Al take a seat, like all those other times.

Al's lips twitched. The old man would probably love it if Sandy got kidnapped and disappeared forever.

He raked the blurriness from his eyes. Trucks were already driving away, with others filing up for their turns on the dirt road. Men still surrounded Billy Bob. Al counted, then counted twice, got twelve the first time, fourteen the second, including Billy Bob. His gun hand trembled. He didn't stand a chance.

He clapped his left hand around the gun. The two-handed grip banished the shakes. He aimed at Billy Bob. Killing the boss might make the entire criminal operation collapse, once and for all. He let his arms fall while maintaining the two-handed grip. He pressed the gun's butt into his thigh. He surveyed the stragglers. They were probably drawing straws to see who got dibs as they took cracks at Sandy.

Redness flooded in and tunneled his field of vision. Kadaski, Sampson, Mosca, and all the others flocking around their master, at one time or another over the years, he'd caught the pervs leering at Sandy's boobs, or her ass. They were probably slobbering all over themselves to get at her. Billy Bob was probably dangling her as a prize, for who could smuggle the most drugs, and who could traffic the most victims. If he blitzed, took out Billy Bob and some of his inner circle, the rest of the cowards were sure to scatter. Then he could break Sandy out of the cabin.

He lifted the gun. He squinted his right eye. If he missed … he released the gun with his left hand and swiped his forearm over his sweaty, gritty forehead, heading off the sweat trickling from his greasy hair. He re-gripped the gun, which slid a little under the pressure. He passed the gun from one hand to the other as he wiped his palms on his jeans. He sighted Billy Bob. If he missed, Billy Bob's goons would surely gun him down.

He lowered the gun again, resting its butt against his thigh. He could run off. They'd never find him. He could get the cops. His head spasmed. Billy Bob owned the cops. If he didn't do something, right the fuck now, then Sandy was doomed. After Billy Bob's minions got sick of gang-raping her, they'd smuggle her down to Mexico, or further south, or maybe over to Japan, or Bangkok, or wherever they could sell her. She'd live out the rest of her days in brutal half-darkness, which would deepen as she deteriorated, commanding an ever-decreasing price, drugged and beaten into submission, infested with diseases, one of which would surely kill her. He couldn't stand idly by and let the mother of his ...

He fired, and fired, and fired. The gun clicked empty.

Bullets pelted the trees around him. Slugs sent up splinters, whanged off bark, drove him down to his belly. He covered the back of his skull with both hands. He wriggled across the row toward the next line of trees.

A slew of commands to stop, to freeze, preceded the kneecap crushing into his kidneys, and the hands grabbing his wrists and wish-boning his arms.

"What should we do with him?"

Knuckles ground into the side of his face and mashed his head into the grass. Jeaned legs and boots clogged his sight line.

"Jesus H. Christ."

Billy Bob's voice froze Al. He'd failed, and now he was gonna die. He'd blown his last chance to get it right, his last chance to be worthy ... He sobbed, "I'm sorry."

Billy Bob growled, "You're gonna be, boy."

Chapter Twenty

"There's not much daylight left," Hennig said. "Let's get a move on."

While preparing to open the next Plexiglas chamber containing a killer queen, Sandy damned his head-to-toe suit for obscuring almost all his non-verbal cues. His muffled, businesslike monotone baffled her. They only had a few trays to go before they finished these hives. Wouldn't be long until he locked her up for the night. The thought of being shackled with her arms stretched over her head all night long intensified the ache in her low back and shoulders. Maybe, since she didn't run off when she had the chance, he'd grant her a little more freedom, a little more comfort. She was dying to question him, but she didn't want to screw up what good will she'd built up by being too nosy, by making him suspect that the urge to discover his plan was the thing that made her stay.

She used the slender, stainless steel tongs to capture the queen, which wriggled as she handed the tongs to him. The reddish-orange sunlight reflected off his black visor. For all she knew, this could be the wrap-up. she might not get another shot. As she cleared her throat, she reminded herself not to ask a direction question. *Keep it casual.* "Seems like a waste of time. Everybody's so worried about CCD that they're gonna go over every tray with a fine toothed comb. One look and they're gonna know these giants aren't their bees."

She held her breath. Hennig took the tongs from her and bent back to an open tray. He placed the queen into the hive and eased the tray shut. Without swiveling toward her, he reached the tongs toward her. "One ..." She jumped a little at the sound of his voice, then took the tongs from him. "... beekeepers are looking for CCD. When they see a bustling, healthy hive, they will move on without further scrutiny, relieved to find no signs of the affliction. Two, those who do notice ..." He hesitated while opening the next tray, "... will be so devastated by the possibility of the loss of their business – think of your husband's situation – that they will hide the fact that their bees have been replaced." He extracted the tray's queen and dropped the gassed bee into the pouch on his belt. "They will not dare to mention it to their peers – again, look what happened at the merest hint of CCD in your husband's case – and thus they will keep

78

themselves in the dark, hoping that the problem will go away on its own, hoping that these replacement bees will do a suitable job of pollinating, which, they will not, a fact that they will discover far too late."

She handed him the tongs, another killer queen squirming between the pincers. "So you ruin this year's almond crop. So what? How does that further your aim to convince the world of global warming?" Behind her visor, she bit her lip. The question got out before she could stop it. No matter how many different angles she explored, she kept coming back to this motive. Now, if he didn't correct her, or mock her, or do something to indicate that she was wrong …

"The Almond Chase is the epicenter of commercial beekeeping in the US, and to make up for the CCD-driven honeybee shortfall, almond producers offer top dollar to have hives shipped in from all over the world. From the Valley, hives will travel all over the country, so that my bees will mingle with the hives of nearly every other commercial beekeeper in the nation, and, don't forget those foreign hives returning to their native lands. One of the many genetic modifications of my bees is the ability to reproduce at a rapid rate–"

Hennig raised a white-gloved finger. Sandy pinpointed an engine's distant rumble. Had to be the trailer's tenant approaching along the dirt road.

"Returning ahead of schedule," Hennig said.

Sandy pursed her lips. More like they tried to squeeze too much in to get back on schedule.

"Pack it up," Hennig said. "Quickly!"

She rushed the loaded dolly past the first row of trees, then Hennig called a halt. Headlight beams preceded the ramshackle red pickup, which lurched to a stop in front of the trailer. Sandy didn't recognize the truck's lone occupant, but his scuffed boots, faded jeans, flannel shirt, and trucker's cap were standard, off-duty beekeeper gear. The man, carrying a rifle, went straight into the trailer. Window by window, lights flicked on, marking his progress from one end of the trailer to the other. Sandy fumed out a shallow breath. Hennig might've told her everything if this jerk hadn't barged in. Now she'd have to start over from square one and hope she could steer him back towards full disclosure.

Hennig hissed. He pointed toward the hives. She'd left the small white duffel on top of one of the hive bodies.

She thumped the side of her fist into her thigh while whispering, "Shoot."

Hennig breathed, "Go get it. *Now!*"

She flinched. She scrambled, nearly tripped over her own feet, Francis' suit billowed and bunched around her smaller dimensions, making her clumsy.

Hennig's left hand clamped around her upper arm. With his right hand he jabbed his gun's muzzle into her ribs. "Don't let him see you. Try anything, I'll be forced to kill the two of you."

His sudden swing toward murderous froze her, except for her face, which flushed so hot that sweat droplets began to trickle down her temples.

He gave her arm an abrupt shake. "*Go!*" He released her.

She hunched. She circled until the wall of hive bodies stood between herself and the trailer. She slunk toward the hives, keeping her eyes on the lighted windows. A dark shape invaded the living room window. She paused on her toes. The dark shape lingered. She couldn't tell if he was holding his rifle, but she could imagine how she'd look to him, skulking around his hives in her space-age white beekeeper suit. Maybe Hennig was right in assuming that beekeepers wouldn't notice the imposter queens, or, if they did, they wouldn't dare speak up about them. Or maybe the man was going around armed with a rifle because they all knew that somebody was monkeying around with their bees.

The shape whisked away from the window. Could be a trick. From the trees behind her, Hennig growled. She trembled. She took a deep breath, exhaled slow until her body stilled. She resumed her painstaking pace.

She reached the hive body. She grazed the duffel with her glove's fingerpads, then she inched her hand away from the bag. She estimated less than ten seconds to dash to the trailer's front door. An unexpected sprint, twilight, a handgun, Hennig would probably miss the shot. The man inside had a gun, and had to have a phone. All they would have to do was hunker down until the cops came.

Her stomach acids churned. What if he could really convince the entire world of the reality of global warming? No wonder he got so pissed off at her. He'd sacrificed everything for this cause. She couldn't imagine the indignities he'd suffered while maintaining his mask, while always working his way deeper into the belly of the beast. What if he could really pull it off, but in a moment of weakness she ruined the whole thing?

She grabbed the duffel. She had nothing left to lose by helping him. She might just help him save the world. She hustled back to the trees. She circled back to him. She whispered, "I got it."

He waved the gun toward the dolly. She placed the bag on top of the ceramic containers. She placed her foot on the lower crossbar and levered the dolly onto its wheels. She pushed the dolly towards the cart, which they'd hidden several rows away. He marched a few steps directly behind her. She glanced over her shoulder. He kept the gun aimed at her back.

As the dolly's wheels trundled over the rugged ground, she searched for something to say. She couldn't help coming back, again and again, to the same point, that she'd proved her trustworthiness twice today. She couldn't come up with a way to say it that didn't feel whiney or insincere. *It wasn't fair.* She blinked away the threat of tears. It wasn't fair.

His silence continued. She bared her teeth. Maybe she was jumping to conclusions. Maybe he wasn't trying to save the world. The dolly's load jounced over a hard bump. She realized she'd been stalking faster. His stony silence made deceleration hard, made thinking straight harder.

When they reached the cart he watched her load up their equipment. Once she secured the dolly, she took a breath in preparation to speak her mind.

"I've gone too far to turn back," he said. "One stupid mistake could ruin everything, make all my efforts a waste."

"I'm sorry." The words, the bashful tone, escaped her lips before she could swallow them.

With the gun he directed her toward the passenger seat. He slid behind the wheel, still pointing the gun at her, still wearing his helmet. She wished he would take it off so she could see his face.

He started the cart. "You're not stupid. Did you leave the bag on purpose?"

"What?"

He firmed his gun arm, aiming at her stomach. "I don't see how I can trust you."

"I–"

"Shut up. I have to think about what I'm going to do with you."

Chapter Twenty-one

The deepening gloom threatened to engulf the unlit bulb overhead. Sandy's back ached from lying on the air mattress all day long. She twisted onto her side, but her concentrated weight caused her hip bone to bottom out against the hard floor, and she could only stand that pain for a few minutes. For the umpteenth time, she lowered her shoulders until her shackles, which stretched her arms over her head, tautened against the eyebolt. She could feel it. She could tear the eyebolt right out of the wall. Maybe she could work the bolt back into place before he returned.

She stared at the closed blinds. If he'd hid a video camera in the room, he'd have planted the lens on the adjuster rod, or maybe up in the housing. The bare, dirty white walls, the threadbare gray carpet, there was nowhere else in the room to secrete such devices. He might've sewn a GPS beacon into her clothes, *his clothes*, the jeans and tee-shirt smelled like his expensive lemongrass soap. He, or his henchman, might be waiting outside. If she did rip free from the wall, she had to commit to making a run for it, one hundred percent. He'd be back any second now. Then the decision would be out of her hands.

She exhaled slow through her nose. Say she did escape. What did she have to go back to? Divorce, certainly. She was not gonna live in that house with those two frigid men a second longer. The truth was, Al had run the business into the ground. She wasn't gonna get much, if anything, alimony-wise. She'd have to get a job, which was gonna make it double tough to keep going to school.

Her lips contorted. She snorted, "School." She wasn't exactly getting the college experience. The kids, the *teenagers*, she heard them whispering, laughing at her behind her back, making fun of her because she was older, and already far, far behind them, career-wise. Working fulltime, schooling part-time, she'd be in her late-thirties, most likely, by the time she got her PhD, and was ready to start her practice. She'd be in debt up to her eyeballs. The image she'd constructed of her older, successful self, Doctor James (she'd tried to go back, find the point when she began to use her maiden name in this dream, but she couldn't find the precise moment), the black-framed glasses, the tasteful yet flattering shoulder-length hairdo, the notebook, the plush chairs, the patient sitting across from her, the warm, wood-paneled office, the path to this ideal seemed more narrow, more fraught with pitfalls than ever.

The distant throb of an impending headache warned her to relax her brow. He'd made vague hints about what came 'After.' He'd implied he might have a place for her, but he was even more vague about what that place might be. She didn't have the credentials, or the experience, to be a lab assistant, or anything like that. He wasn't married. As far as she knew he didn't have a girlfriend. But he seemed to be bending over backwards to give her chances to prove herself. When he'd returned in the afternoon, to feed her, to give her water, and to let her use the bathroom, he'd said, 'I wish I could trust you. I could sure use your help, but I can't take the chance that you'll betray me when I'm so close to realizing my goal.' The memory made her wince, but she couldn't blame him for not trusting her. If she could go back and do it again she'd make damn sure to grab that bag. She'd just been in such a rush to get to the trees before that beekeeper caught them.

She frowned. She hadn't done it on purpose. Not consciously, anyways. But subconsciously, in the heat of the moment … maybe her subconscious desires rose up and seized the opportunity. Maybe subconsciously, she didn't believe him. Maybe deep down she thought he was a madman, and if she stuck around, he'd kill her as soon as he was done with her. Didn't working the bolt loose prove that?

Her frown deepened. That lurking headache stirred again, but she couldn't relax. Maybe she didn't forgive him for Mikey. She'd told herself she did, especially after he forgave her, even claimed she was justified, for killing Francis. But maybe somewhere down in her lower brain functions, her primal instinct was to murder him, to get revenge.

She ground her teeth. Maybe this was the true test, the rising above her base, animalistic urges. Mikey's death could have meaning, if she could rise above those urges, and help this man save the world.

The cart's soft putt penetrated the trailer's walls. She sighed. She relaxed. She relaxed further at the sound of the trailer's front door opening. His light footsteps hurried straight to her room. She emptied her lungs. He wasn't gonna let her languish.

He opened the door and flicked on the light. She squinted against the sudden brightness. His back seemed slightly stooped. Circles sagged the skin under his eyes. He said, "How are you?"

The upsurge of relief blindsided her, almost brought tears to her eyes before she choked it down. In a meek tone, she managed to say, "Fine."

He came to her, and, without taking any pains to guard against attack, he went to work on her shackles.

She blurted, "I couldn't help it …"

He shushed her. He unlocked her and helped her sit up. She groaned. She swooned. He caught her, waited for her to regain her wits, then levered her up to her feet. He said, "Walk around, get your blood flowing. Then go ahead and take a long hot shower. There's clean towels in the bathroom closet. I'll dig you up some clean clothes."

She hesitated. She searched his green eyes. She tottered out of the door and turned towards the bathroom. Once inside, she locked the door, then braced herself for his protest. Several heartbeats later, she looked up at the small window. Its crank would open its three slats. She'd have to remove the whole apparatus to squeeze through to the outside. *Don't be stupid.*

She pulled back the shower curtain and turned on the hot water.

Chapter Twenty-two

Al jerked awake. The pain behind his brow swelled to excruciating, forcing a moan out him, then receded, before resurging to excruciating, the intensity squeezing tears from his slitted eyes. The multitude of aches and pains pinging up and down his muscles and joints filled the valleys of that brutal throbbing.

"Rhodes! Get off your lazy ass."

Al dragged his forearm across his eye sockets. The unbroken gray crystallized into masonry and iron bars. He inhaled. The astringent tang of industrial cleansers did not mask the underlying whiff of unwashed males. Al swallowed his gorge.

"Rhodes! On your feet!"

Al closed him mouth against a series of wet belches. The cop looked pissed off. He lurched to his feet, placed a palm on the slightly gummy wall to steady himself. "What's going on?"

"Your ugly ass is bailed out. Now let's get a move on!"

Al shaded his eyes as he staggered down the too bright hallway. From behind, the cop paced him, nudging him along when Al doddered too close to the wall. With each step, Al's stride grew more sure, and he blinked his eyesight clearer, increasing the overlap of his double vision. By the time they'd reached the door to the parking lot, he was more or less seeing straight.

The nighttime chill provoked goosebumps. Al shivered. Only a few cars occupied slots in the parking lot. Billy Bob leaned his backside against the shiny grill of his big black F150. He crossed one jeaned leg over the other, the tip of that cowboy boot pointing up in the air. His arms folded across his chest, each fist tucked into the crook of its opposite arm, his bony elbows stretched the fabric of his checkered flannel. Under the brim of his garish cowboy hat, his hard eyes caught the lamplight and glittered.

"He's all yours," the cop said. The metal door banged shut behind Al.

"I had to call in just about every chit owed to me to spring you. I had to tell them you got skunked on account of your son."

Al flinched.

"C'mon, get in the truck, I'll drive ya home." Billy Bob pushed himself off the grill and swaggered to the driver's door. His heels created a gritty *tock* against the tarmac.

Al couldn't move.

Billy Bob regarded Al for a moment, then clapped his hands. The sharp smack made Al jump. "Hop to it! Gonna be daylight soon, time to get to work. I've already wasted too much time and energy on your crazy shit."

Al limped to the truck. Both his hips and knees ached. He got in the cab as Billy Bob started the engine. He settled into his seat. The truck rocked a little in exiting the parking lot, each sway making Al a little woozier. He focused on the dense, pulsing disc of pain above his eyes, and on careful breathing, to keep from puking. His efforts ate up a few ticks down the darkened two-lane highway.

"Lemme know if you're gonna puke," Billy Bob said, "so I can pull over."

Al shook his head. He suppressed a burp, then said, "I'm gonna be okay." He wasn't so sure, though. His couldn't think straight. His awareness felt syrupy and slow, and he couldn't control its direction, or stop its blobby momentum. He couldn't find any clarity in the past few nights' events, other than a mounting sense of shame. He didn't know how he'd be able to show his face around here, or back home, or anywhere, ever again.

"Yeah," Billy Bob said. "You'll be all right. Just gotta let this shitstorm blow over. Regroup. Take some time, get your head on straight."

Al's tension loosened a mote. "Got that right." He exhaled, and the constriction in his chest relaxed with his breath. "You heard anything about Sandy?"

Billy Bob grunted. "We gotta get your bees out. With those tarps up, those blooms will go to waste otherwise. I'll help you with that, but then you need to get some rest."

Al was about to ask again, but Billy Bob's arm flashed out. Al cringed. Billy Bob flicked on the radio. At low volume, classic country music filled the cab. Billy Bob sat back and said, "We'll put all this mess behind us, get back to work. But once you fulfill your contract here, you oughtta think about heading straight home."

Al nodded. A gaping yawn surprised him, nearly unhinged his jaw. He was so tired. He'd love to go to sleep in his own bed.

The hum of the tires, the Ford's finely-turned engine, the gentle music, all combined to make his eyelids droop. He was so tired.

Something jostled Al awake. His closed eyelids glowed red. He eased them open, averting his gaze from sun. He stared at Billy Bob's cowboy hat, the silver diamond pattern on the black band, Billy Bob's longish gray hair sticking out the back, then jail, the parking lot, and the haze looming behind those events, roared back into the center of his thoughts. He tried to speak but nothing came out. He cleared his phlegmy throat and said, "Where are we?"

Billy Bob kept his eyes on the road. "Gotta check on something real quick-like. Don't worry, it's on the way."

Al didn't recognize this stretch of road, but then again, the pinkish-white orchards all looked pretty much the same.

Billy Bob drummed his hairy fingers on the steering wheel. "You know you and Sven aren't the only ones them bees got to. Got so bad, I called in an expert."

Al closed his eyes. He imagined a pale round face, receding, short red hair, devious green eyes, and a hint of a smile playing over thin lips. He opened his eyes. "Hennig, right?"

"How'd you know?"

Al shrugged.

"He took one look around and said it must be feral bees." Billy Bob snorted. "Cost me a pretty penny for that expert opinion."

Billy Bob took his boot off the gas and flipped the turn signal on. He guided the Ford off the highway and onto a dirt road, which twisted into the orchards. "I mean he didn't just turn around and fly back to Hollywood, or wherever the hell he spends his time, Vegas probably." Billy Bob winked at Al. "He stayed in the field, 'collecting specimens,' he claimed."

Al caught hold of a flicker of running into Hennig. In the field, yes, but the rest was murky. He strained to dredge up any detail. Billy Bob turned the Ford off the dirt road and onto the grass between rows of almond trees. Branches scraped the Ford, some bending all the way forward before whipping back into place behind the truck. Al frowned. He thought he remembered Hennig warning him about Billy Bob.

Al willed himself not to stare at Billy Bob. The harder he tried to remember exactly what Hennig said, the harder his head throbbed. Sweat slicked his forehead. Ahead, a pair of rickety white hive bodies obstructed the row.

Billy Bob parked the Ford a good twenty yards from the hive bodies.

Al ran his tongue around the inside of his dry mouth. He croaked, "Where are we?"

"Don't pretend like you don't know."

Al spotted a beat up ATV wedged between trees a few paces behind the hive bodies. "I don't–"

"At first I thought you'd just gone plain nuts, what with Sandy fixin' to leave you, and then what happened to Mikey ..."

Al tensed. He growled, "Don't you–"

"... but then I find out you knew what you were doin' all along."

Al's confusion chilled his rage. Before he could demand to know what the hell was going on, Billy Bob said, "Oh, I knew it was you right off the bat. Always digging and snooping, you and your goddamned conspiracy theories. The way Elmer described you, you sounded like some kind of monster, but underneath the stings, yeah, I knew he was talking about our former fair-haired boy."

Al winced.

"I didn't know how you found out that I got them Minutemen-wannabe boys to do some of my dirty work, but in hindsight, you must've figured it out, on account of you had everything else already figured out. Or maybe one of those scumbag illegals told you. I don't care either way anymore."

Al's mind accelerated, stumbling over the events of the last few nights, snagging on flashes of bound men, gunplay, human trafficking, gun running, drug smuggling ... he murmured, "The CIA covers your ass."

Without showing his teeth, Billy Bob grinned. "Them boys owe me going way back. But I guess you know all about that shit." He lifted a handgun from between his thigh and the driver's door. He aimed at Al's guts. "Get out of the truck."

"You're gonna kill me?"

"Get out of the goddamned truck."

"The cops know I left with you."

"Boy, you been on a rampage, shooting at innocent folk, scaring the shit out of people all across the valley, what with your stung-up face. All they're gonna ask me is when I last saw you, and all I gotta say is I dropped you off at your trailer. If I gotta, I'll shoot you right here. Now get out of the damned truck!"

Al snuck a look at the trees. He eased out of the truck. He expected Billy Bob to get out on the other side. He figured his only shot was to run for it. He dipped in preparation. Billy Bob leaned over and pulled the passenger door shut. Al watched Billy Bob run his fingers around the window's seal.

Al scowled. In the silence, between his harsh breaths, an angry buzzing grew louder. He said, "Aw, shit ..."

The pivoted his back to the swarm as the first bees pelted him. He saw bees coating the Ford's nose before he slapped his palms over his eyes. He heard the Ford's engine scream before the buzzing filled his ears. Al dropped to the grass and curled into the fetal position. The strafe of tiny stabs scattered any concern for Billy Bob's accusations. Numbness flooded up his limbs and into his brain.

Chapter Twenty-three

Sandy let her eyes go out of focus. The almond petals smeared into a pinkish-white blur. Hennig piloted the cart down the precise center of the row, maintaining a buffer of at least half a foot from the reach of the longest low branches. The cart's speed created a draft that gave a gentle lift to her clean hair, as well as providing a steady stream of the blossoms' sweet fragrance. Soon, they would don their helmets and get to work.

She glanced at him. He had that faraway look in his eyes. She'd been waiting for him to say something, waiting for an opening, but he'd been quiet all morning. Not mean, just deep within himself. She couldn't think of any other way to prompt him into opening up about his plans, and about what came after, so, fearing that pretty soon they'd be working and the opportunity for casual conversation long gone, she said, "We must almost be done with this part of it." She held her breath. She itched for him to talk about the next stage of his plan, or, if this was the final stage, what her role would be afterwards.

"From here the imposter bees will be transported all over the country, and all over the world."

She maintained a placid exterior, but she allowed herself an inward groan. He'd already told her this, over and over again. She could almost predict his exact phrasing as he locked into his lecture on how his genetically modified bees would quickly spread throughout the international community of commercial beekeepers. From there he deviated into his favorite tangent and expounded on gene splicing and mutation until his technobabble dizzied her.

"This concentration of artificial supersedure will result in the seemingly total extinction of honeybees."

She sniffed. Her ears perked as she straightened her spine.

"CCD has already crippled the industry. The predator bees will accelerate the tipping point, and the entire house of cards will come crashing down."

His white-gloved hands made a slight adjustment on the steering wheel. She squeezed the edges of her seat cushion. He'd never before spoken so far down this line of thought. Of course she'd tested her way to this point, but she'd always dead-ended, unable to make any clear connection between the extinction of honeybees and global warming. She'd ruminated on the possibility that honeybees were a keystone species, but there'd been scads of other endangered species, none of which moved mainstream sentiments toward any dire conclusions.

He took his foot off the gas pedal. The cart slowed. Not far ahead the row widened to a small clearing, which contained a camper and tent combo. One of Billy Bob's bargain-basement plots. Al had tried to talk her into renting one of these no-electricity, no-water camps in order to cut costs, but she had insisted on a trailer, especially with Mikey along … she bowed her head.

He stopped the cart. She stepped out of the shade of the almond trees and into the sizzling rays of the morning sun. Sweat droplets broke out on her forehead. She gazed at the hive bodies. The slats hung crooked, rickety, the hives the saddest she'd ever seen. She could imagine these poor people striving to keep their business afloat, hanging on by their fingernails. Hennig's predator bees would destroy them. She felt sick.

"The only way," Hennig said, "to truly impact everyday people is to affect the quality and quantity of the food on their dinner plates."

She reeled toward him. The heat made the air shimmer.

"I am merely accelerating the inevitable results of CCD."

"Then what?" Her voice sounded thick and distant to herself. She took a deep breath and concentrated on his words.

"I have a secure method of both eradicating this strain of bees and reviving the honeybee population. I have the means to resurrect the industry, albeit in a sustainable way. The apparent extinction of honeybees causes a two-fold benefit: the eradication of CCD, a clear and present danger that needs to be dealt with immediately in any case, and the restructuring of the pollination industry in a sustainable fashion. It will wipe the slate clean, a do-over. But this is not the main thrust, more of a fringe benefit, albeit a very important benefit. No, the main …

Blackness swirled in, shrinking her vision to pinprick. Her legs folded underneath her and she slumped down to the grass. She lolled, rolling her head back and forth. His shadow blocked the sun, cooled her face. He dabbed a wetted cloth on her forehead, then her lips. He worked his arm beneath her back and raised her, her head settling into the crook of his elbow. Her eyelids fluttered. She couldn't make out the words he spoke, but his tone soothed her. She relaxed into his strong embrace. He held his canteen to her lips long enough for a chest-tingling sip.

The darkness receded to spots across her field of vision. She inhaled lemongrass-lime, the scent of his soap.

He leaned in close to her and breathed, "Are you okay?"

The spots swirled, expanding and contracting in time with her heartbeat. She closed her eyes and raised her mouth. Her lips brushed smooth skin. She opened her eyes. He'd turned his lips away, her lips touching his cheek. She recoiled. Her whispered apologies seemed to be lost on him as he hoisted her to her feet.

He propped her up and walked her toward the cart. Her face throbbed hotter and hotter all the way. She wanted to curl up and die. He sat her down in the cart, in the shade, and helped her get her helmet on.

"Sit here," he said. "Drink some water. You've been working too hard."

She was glad that the helmet hid her burning cheeks, gladder still when he put his helmet on and moved back towards the hives. She'd give anything to take it back. She couldn't see how she could look him in the eyes. He'd never take her seriously now, not after she acted like a lovesick schoolgirl. He was probably already revising his plans for her after all this business was over. She looked down at her white boots, unable to even watch him as he went to work.

She curled her hands into fists and squeezed as hard as she could. She gave her head a single violent shake. *Stupid.*

She exhaled. She uncurled her fists. She'd fainted right before he was about to spill the beans. She scrolled back, tried to remember what he said, something about the collapse of the honeybee industry hitting everyday people's dinner plates.

She frowned, but she felt like she was faking it, like her shame was bubbling up from underneath. *Fake it till you make it.* Her face still burned, but she forced herself to process this new information. She knew that the extinction of honeybees would impact the production of certain foods, but people would still be able to get their doughnuts and potato chips.

She crossed her arms over her chest. The public might blame the pesticide industry for both the extinction of honeybees and the mutant killer bees. Everybody knew that pesticides didn't kill all their targeted pests, and the survivors bred stronger, more resilient pests. Maybe he was trying to create a tipping point, the loss of honeybees making workaday people review and rethink their current opinions across the entire spectrum of issues pertaining to the environment. Maybe the public backlash would be so overwhelming that big agriculture would change its practices. Maybe such a success would encourage and energize left-leaning people in regards to climate-change issues.

She peered at him. Her guesses were reaches, at best. He was risking everything, coming out into the open after years of playing the rightwing stooge. His plan had to be more solid in order to justify such a risk. Knowing him, his plan would leave nothing to chance.

She adjusted her helmet. She stood up. She wasn't gonna figure it out sitting in the shade while he worked. She took a ginger step, then let her muscles steady themselves. She strode toward him, each step stronger and faster than the last. She had to show him that she was worthy of learning exactly how they were gonna change the world.

Chapter Twenty-four

Sandy reduced the speed of her chewing to a crawl. After her shower, he had dinner ready, zesty chicken breast, steamed broccoli seasoned with a light oil, and for desert, fresh chunks of red Bartlet pear, the juicy fruit nearly melting in her mouth and making her attempt to dawdle near impossible. 'A super-healthy meal,' he explained, and he'd said little else since. She'd managed a few mumbled compliments on his cooking prowess. She sensed that he meant to bring up this morning's indiscretion as soon as they finished eating. She was down to her last chunk of pear. She hadn't yet come up with a good response. The fatigue finally got to her. She could tell him that, but she couldn't bring herself to tell him how long, how very, very long it had been since anyone had held her in a gentle, caring way. She literally couldn't say for sure. She couldn't remember the last time Al had touched her, might even be as long as a year, maybe even longer. Just the perfect storm, everything going wrong at the right time. She couldn't have feelings for him. *She didn't have feelings for him.*

She swallowed, speared the last chunk of pear with her fork, and glanced across the kitchen table toward him as she shoveled the fruit into her mouth. A receding hairline. Sparse, and obviously artificially-stimulated red stubble filling in the bald spot on top of his head. Almost exactly her height, tall for a woman, but below average for a man. Yeah, he kept his body lean, but normally she wouldn't give him a second look. The only remarkable thing about him was the super intelligence crackling out of his intense green eyes.

He caught her staring. She blushed and lowered her gaze to her bowl. She muttered, "I'll clear the dishes." She wanted to do something, anything to escape those laser beam eyes. She rose from her chair.

He raised a hand. "I'll get them later. Right now, we need to talk."

She settled back into her seat.

She tried to will herself to make eye contact, but she could only muster a quick peek before staring at her hands, which she'd folded in her lap. A flicker of hope, that he might finally clarify his plan and her role afterwards, lifted her spirits, then the utter certainty, that he would reprimand her for her attempt to kiss him, plunged her into unbroken darkness. She trembled. She clasped her hands until she stabilized herself.

"You're an apparently healthy twenty-six year old women," Hennig said. "True, you've endured a great deal of physical stress, and even more psychological stress, which can manifest itself physically. But just to be on the safe side, in order to be certain that your fainting spell is not symptomatic of a serious underlying problem, I'd like to examine you, with your permission, of course."

She realized that her chin had dropped to the point of gaping, so she snapped her mouth shut. She basked in the cooling wave of relief, which allowed her to raise her head and meet his gaze. "You earned an MD too?"

He chuckled. "No, no, just a few PhD's. But I have some medical training, enough to do a cursory checkup, enough to detect any obvious anomalies in your vital systems. Better safe than sorry. So …?"

She nodded.

In the living room he dragged the one comfy chair, the one with the padded arms, a few feet away from the wall. When she took his outstretched hand, his gentle grip sent a slight tingle up her spine as he guided her to the chair. After he seated her he headed into the hallway, towards his bedroom.

She caught herself appraising his butt. She looked down at the brown carpet. *What am I doing? Stupid.* Acting like a teenybopper the first time a man touched her. She'd gone over it and over it ever since this morning's embarrassment. His intelligence, certainly, was unlike any she'd ever experienced before. His brilliance almost beamed out of his eyes. But it was more than that. He was gentle, considerate, even kind. But on top of that, he was trying to save the world. He'd sacrificed everything to try to save the world. She'd never met anybody like him, not even close, not even in the same universe. He was nothing like the monosyllabic, self-obsessed brooder she'd married, the man who with each passing moment, and day, and year, had devolved into more of a stranger. Their marriage had twisted into the exact opposite of how a marriage was supposed to work. With the perspective that just these few days of distance had granted, her old life seemed so very bizarre.

He toted a black medical bag into the living room. A stethoscope jounced around his neck. "I'm pretty sure that stress is the root the cause of your spell." He placed the bag beside the chair and opened it. "I apologize. Sometimes, I grow so focused on the task at hand that I forget the extremes my carelessness forced you into, simply to defend yourself. In case you are burdened by any guilt regarding Francis, I want to assure you, the blame is one hundred percent mine. I should have never allowed you to be trapped in such a position."

She didn't know what to say, so she said, "Thank you." The truth was, the only times she thought about killing Francis were the times she was surprised that she hardly thought about it at all. She suspected subconscious repression, that one day the enormity would spring up in full force, perhaps manifest physically in the form of a tumor.

"Also, unforgivably, your recent loss slips my mind. Your grief must still be so raw. Once again, I want to express my condolences for the death of your son, and I hope that someday you will forgive me for pressing you into … *service*, when you should be taking care of yourself, when you should be working on healing yourself."

She sniffled. A series of rapid blinks freed a tear from her eye. She bowed her head.

He placed his index finger under her jaw and the ball of his thumb on her chin, then eased her head upwards until their eyes met. Sadness dampened his green eyes. "I'm just so sorry that he was even there at all." He shifted his hand to her cheek, let his palm linger on her skin, then his hand dropped away.

A soft hitch marred her inhale. She recalled that night, the gloomy, drafty kitchen, Al insisting that Mikey come along, the old man, stony, implacable, looming behind Al, the two of them demanding that Mikey's future lied in the family business. She ground her teeth. That recollection seared away the threat of more teardrops. The two of them, pressuring her, no, that wasn't right, *assuming* that their word was law. Then *after*, just a hiccup of a funeral before getting right back to the goddamned family business. Wasting time on a failing business, instead of taking a moment to grieve, taking some time to rethink things, maybe try to do some good, maybe try to honor Mikey's memory.

He stepped behind her and massaged her shoulders. "Clear your mind. Deep breaths. Relax."

She inhaled the lemongrass-lime scent of his soap. He must've washed up while she was in the shower. A moan of pleasure snuck out of her before she could swallow it. The realization that his position behind her kept him from seeing her latest blush soothed her to somewhere near to poise. She anticipated the withdrawal of his hands and so prevented what would've been a disappointed groan.

He fished a penlight out of the medical bag and switched it on. He leaned in front of her and said, "Follow my finger." He cruised his finger back and forth while shining the light in one eye, then the other. "Good, looks good."

"Are you sure my brain's not broken?"

He let out a quiet laugh while placing the penlight back in the bag. "Your cognitive functions seem physically sound. But you're the Psych major. I'll leave those types of judgements up to you."

He stood at her shoulder. "Tilt your head back a little." He laid his palms on the sides of her neck and applied the barest hint of pressure.

To distract herself from her elevated heartbeat, she said, "I don't know anymore. I can't even figure out how honeybee extinction connects to global warming."

He smiled. He removed his hands. "No swelling."

He stooped to the medical bag. She grimaced at the frustration welling up inside her. He was gonna dodge the question again.

He produced a gray tube, pulled off one end, and pivoted toward her, aiming a thermometer at her mouth. "Open up and say 'Ah'." He took great care in wedging the thermometer's tip under her tongue. She clamped her teeth around it.

He rubbed his jaw, then said, "One of the benefits of being a public advocate for the pesticide industry, and big agriculture in general, is access. The disinformation can flow both ways."

She frowned. She surged toward fitting this odd new piece into the puzzle. He pulled a blood-pressure cuff from the medical bag. He cinched the cuff around her right arm and squeezed the little black ball until the cuff was tight. She bit her tongue. She couldn't concentrate. She'd always hated the uncomfortable feel of these things, the tightness on her bicep.

He observed the dial, then said, Good." As he deflated the cuff, he said, "The effectiveness of the rightwing propaganda machine was more deep and more thorough, and hence, more successful, than its architects' wildest dreams." He stowed the cuff in the bag. He faced her and said, "But this resounding success brought unintended consequences. You might have noted the phenomenon of radical, true believers defeating establishment republicans in primaries, then, either losing to their more moderate adversaries in general elections, or, should they win election, their terms are blighted by racial and gender slurs, so as to make re-election unlikely."

She nodded. She had indeed noticed that phenomenon.

He pinched the end of the thermometer. "Okay." She opened her mouth. He glanced at the gauge. "This radicalizing, this conversion has reached even to those who should know better, to the would-be puppet-masters. Inheriting wealth, hiring professionals to administer that wealth, does not require a great deal of penetrating insight."

She smiled.

"Your temperature is normal." He re-tubed the thermometer and tossed it into the bag. "The things I tell the public ... global warming is hoax, a liberal conspiracy. Pesticides, fungicides, herbicides are safe. GMO's are safe ... and all the rest, I assure various industry deciders that these things are indeed true. They want to believe so badly, that even the brighter amongst them accept these assurances. Those that know better, well, the profits are so stupefyingly enormous, they couldn't stop even if they wanted to."

He stood up straight and gestured with the end of the stethoscope. "This works much better against bare skin, so with your permission, if you'd lean a little forward and lift up the back of your shirt ..."

She complied. He stepped closer to her side. He settled his left palm on her shoulder. The coldness of the metal disc made her shiver.

"Take a deep breath."

As she inhaled, she felt the heel of his right palm resting against her bare back. She glanced toward his crotch. She detected no sign of an erection. She pursed her lips. *Are you disappointed?*

He shifted the disc and inch or so and said, "Again."

It dawned on her that he could probably hear her escalating pulse. She tried to use the deep breath to relax. At the end of the exhale, a second ticked by, then he removed his hand and said, "Good." He squared up with her. "Okay, now the front."

Fresh heat billowed into her face. She tilted her head downwards but rolled her eyes upward enough to keep him in full view. She parted her legs, permitting him to move closer. He took a half-step in, but he aimed his eyes at the wall. *Trying to keep it clinical.* This sign that this examination was having at least some affect on him eased her a little.

He reached the stethoscope, still warm from her skin, down the front of her tee-shirt. With his thumb and forefinger he situated the disc on the swell of her left breast. She felt the tips of his three other fingers brush the skin above her bra's cup. Down deep, a tiny tremor caused her heartbeat to stutter. The heat in her face raged anew. Her eyes focused straight ahead at the faded blue-jean expanse of his crotch. Still nothing. She knew when he stepped back, her nipples, hard to the point of throbbing, would show through her worn bra and the thin tee shirt.

"Take a breath."

She almost missed the slight hoarseness in his voice. This evidence, that she wasn't the only one feeling the charged atmosphere, helped her breathe. The oxygen strengthened her, drained some of the weakness from her knees.

"Again."

The second breath cooled her down a smidge, but she remained well above smoldering. She wondered if his request for a second breath was more about drawing out the moment than for function.

"Good." He removed his hand. He tucked the stethoscope into the bag. As he zipped the bag shut, she sagged. The exam was over.

He pivoted and squatted in front of her. "Okay, let me see your right hand."

She held out her right hand. He rotated it and studied her fingernails. He ran his fingertips over hers. "Okay, and now the other."

She extended her left hand. He held it with his right. He lowered her right hand onto her kneecap. His fingertips brushed her thigh, then he took her left with both hands and repeated his inspection. He murmured, "You have strong but graceful hands. Lovely." He slid his right palm under her left, and rubbed the top of her hand with his left. His green gaze blazed into her. "You appear to be in excellent physical condition."

She exhaled, smiled, batted her lashes, then blushed deeper for batting her lashes. She couldn't put two words together.

He gave her hand a light squeeze. "But no more sleeping locked up. Does that sound agreeable to you?"

She felt the sparkling in her eyes. Her voice came out husky when she said, "I'd like that."

Chapter Twenty-five

Distant, faint, then growing louder, finally earsplitting, Al's voice repeated, "No, no, no …"

He jolted awake. He groaned. He imagined cold syrup drenching his brains. He rubbed the shimmer out of his eyesight. Overhead, the moonlight infused the canopy of white blossoms with a translucent glow.

He rolled onto his side, then pushed himself up to his hands and knees. Dark slashes marred the carpet of white blossoms behind him. He recalled the bees bearding the nose of Billy Bob's big black truck, its tires spinning on the grass and the flowers, then catching traction and rocketing backwards down the row.

Billy Bob's accusations flooded back to him. He shook his head, but he couldn't banish the charges, which daisy-chained to the tarps sequestering his plot, and the protests of his peers, like he was Patient Zero of CCD. None of it was true. His bees were healthy. His bees were normal honeybees. This was bullshit. Billy Bob driving him out to this …

He twisted around and waited for the tracers to fade from his vision. His eyes focused on the hive bodies. He stood up too fast and a massive headrush staggered him. He weaved towards the hives. He leaned on the closest body and bowed his head. He sucked in giant breaths, which re-ignited the headrush. He sagged to his knees, closed his eyes, and rested his forehead against the rough wood.

His hands felt puffy and clumsy, but the wood's familiar texture impelled them to fumble over the silent hive. With every fondled inch his fingers gained dexterity. His right hand stopped over a crosshatching of deep scars. Somebody had tried to destroy it, but his fingers traced the stamped impression of the Rhodes' Bees logo.

"No way."

He clutched the top corners of the hive body and hoisted himself to his feet. He opened his eyes. The ass-end of an ATV poked into the row a few trees down. He stomped once toward the ATV and pins and needles erupted in his foot. He yipped, then pigeon-toed it over to the beat-up three-wheeler.

102

He rummaged through the cheap plasticky set of superstore saddlebags. He found a flashlight that he had to whack to get working. He dug up a small black case, which he laid out on the three-wheeler's seat. He unfastened the clasps and shined the weak beam on the strapped-in series of stoppered test-tubes, each tube containing viscous liquid. He studied the dozen or so tubes. He scratched his arm, then returned to the saddlebags. He discarded a screwdriver, an all-in-tool, and then, underneath a thick wad of rags, his hand closed around smooth wood.

He drew his hand out of the saddle bag and held the object under the light. A carved figurine, a beekeeper in old-fashioned gear. His great-grandfather had whittled the figurine, and handed the keepsake down to his son, and so on, and his old man bestowed it upon him when he was five, and before they left on this goddamned trip he …

Al's knees buckled. He melted down to the ground, clutching the toy, mumbling, "It can't be, it can't be."

Thick leather hissing out of the loops of faded blue jeans drew Al's attention outward. He scrunched his eyelids shut and said, "No."

From high above him, his old man said, "You owe me a whippin', boy."

"You're not here, you can't be here."

Whap!

Al flinched. He knew that sound well. His old man doubling up the big brown belt, then those gnarled fists gripping the belt, with a nub sticking out at the end of each hand. A slow inward shift, so that the sections of belt bulged into a big oval between his hands, then faster than Al could blink, snapping both hands out so that the belt lashed against itself. *Whap*! The awful prelude to a beating.

Smack!

Al howled while arching his back. Tears wavered his vision as he opened his eyes. His old man loomed over him, larger than life, the big brown belt dangling from his right fist. Al's back throbbed along the belt's region of contact. His voice cracked while saying, "What are you doing in California?"

"Cleaning up your messes, like always."

"I didn't do it."

"Wish I had a nickel every time you said that."

His old man's hard-bitten features softened as he performed a mimicry of Al's pitch, whining, "I didn't do it ... it's not my fault." His eyes went flinty, his jaw squared, and he said, "Heck, you screwed up every damned time. Every chance you got, you went the wrong way, down the wrong road. Like when you washed out as a ballplayer. The whole town was pulling for you and you let everybody down."

"I couldn't hit a curveball."

His old man's eyes flared. "You didn't try hard enough!"

Al cringed. "I got good grades, though, I got a college degree, which is a lot more than you ever did."

"Yeah, you did good in school, but they're just gonna use that against you."

Al bared his teeth, then shut his mouth, the corners of his lips drooping.

His old man, so tall that Al had to crane his neck to see his chest, said, "Who's to say they aren't right? We did it the same way for four generations, never had no trouble. Then you come back with your fancy degree and your new-fangled ideas, and you ruin everything. Run the business right into the ground. Who's to say your ideas didn't cause Colony Collapse Disorder? I wouldn't be surprised if you screwed up and accidentally bred those killer bees."

"No. I didn't."

"Four generations of work, down the drain. Four generations of building up a business, and you and your ideas take it down–" His old man snapped his fingers, "–like that." His old man planted his fists on his hips, the belt still dangling from his right hand, and said, "They're gonna say you did it all, you and your fancy degree, all the incriminating evidence on your computer, they're gonna say that you were such a screw up that you went crazy ... heck, you were taking potshots at beekeepers. You know how they're gonna spin that, don't you?"

Al drew his knees in, pressing his kneecaps to chest, and he wrapped his arms around his shins. His old man was right.

His old man said, "And what do you think your *loving* wife is gonna tell the cops, the FBI, the reporters, when they come a-calling?"

Al mumbled, "I forgot about her." He raised his head. "Billy Bob–"

"Knock off that crap. Billy Bob don't got her tied up nowhere. You knocked up a piece of white trash, so you had to marry her, then you let her rule the roost. And you think she didn't know about all the pornography on your computer? No wonder she wanted out. She'll be happy to tell the cops and the FBI on you. You know she blames you. For everything."

"Shut up."

"Forget about the family name. Forget about your great-grandfather, your grandfather, me … and you know who … they'll come for miles just to piss on our graves."

A spasm warped through Al's head. He mouthed, "No."

"They're gonna pin all this shit on you."

Al sagged. His eyelids felt so heavy. *What was the use?* "You're right, you're always right. I'm a screw up, always have been."

"They're gonna say your screw up killed Mikey."

With a roar Al sprang to his feet. His old man shriveled to a speck. Al raised his foot and shrieked, "Don't you say his name!" He drove his boot heel down, again and again, again and again, until the shock of his heel slamming into the grass overcame his numbness and the pain attracted bits of his scattered consciousness.

He bent over his knees and panted. His stupid old man was right, they were gonna pin all this shit on him, unless he could figure out who was framing him and clear his name. Show his old man once and for all that he wasn't a screw up.

He squeezed the toy beekeeper, then stuffed it back under the rags. He reloaded the other saddlebag with the tools, first checking the blades on the all-in-one tool. He'd prefer a gun, but beggars couldn't be choosy. He checked the ignition. No keys. He slung the saddlebags over his shoulder and started off. No telling what kind of evidence they planted back at the trailer in his absence.

Chapter Twenty-six

Sandy pivoted too fast and her gloved hand bumped into his. She managed to hold onto the tongs, but the collision caused the killer queen trapped in the pincers to emit an angry buzz. She mumbled, "Sorry."

Hennig took the tongs. "Don't worry about it."

She scrutinized his white, cylindrical helmet, then his full-body white suit, as he returned to the hive body and situated the queen. The space-age gear hid pretty much every signal and cue she might analyze. The lack of indicators sucked, but at least her own suit disguised her recurrent blushes and perspiration. But the suit couldn't mask her jitters, and her persistent clumsiness. She was bumbling like a teenage girl whose body was growing too fast for her to master.

She took a deep breath and commanded herself to relax. Even though she'd read almost none of his body language, she centered on the fact that he'd been unusually quiet throughout the day. When they broke for lunch, instead of his talking about the college courses she'd taken, or discussing the finer points of corporate politics, he'd struggled, made awkward small-talk about the hot weather, and the beauty of the orchards, comparing the petal-strewn ground to pinkish-white snow. This shift in subject matter, from the intellectual to the romantic, had to be significant. After last night, he appeared to be groping his way back to his comfort zone too.

Without turning his black visor her way, he handed the tongs back to her. As she extracted the next queen from its chamber, she cast her mind back to breakfast. She couldn't trust her impressions of his behavior, because her own shyness had raged so intense that she'd withdrawn into herself, narrowing her field of vision, hiding behind her hair. She remembered his hushed tone. He'd made breakfast, done the dishes while she showered. He'd held the door for her when they left the trailer.

She smiled. She could find nothing bad in her impressions. She might not know exactly where his plan was headed, or what would happen afterwards, but she sensed, deep in her bones, that she figured in his life afterwards. She didn't even know if he meant to publicly reveal himself as a closet liberal, or if he meant to continue on as a secret agent, further disrupting the rightwing. But she was certain that he meant to keep her around. She could picture the two of them moving on to the next project, perhaps exposing frakking, or mountaintop mining, or any of a dozen other crucial issues.

"Somebody's coming."

She froze. Over the soft hum of the bees, an engine grumbled. She placed the tongs in the ceramic container and closed the lid. He stepped behind the dolly and levered it back onto its wheels. She gave the hive bodies a rapid once-over, then trotted after him toward the almond trees.

Two rows deep they stopped and slipped behind tree trunks. A red pickup rattled into the clearing and parked in front of the trailer. The driver got out of the truck. On the passenger side, an enormous man squeezed out of the door, his ponderous motion causing the cab to rock. A loose Clippers jersey draped over his red tee shirt. The hems of his blue shorts hung halfway down his shins. The bill of his cap slanted low, shading his eyes. He waddled toward the trailer.

The driver, wearing jeans and a sallow undershirt, strode toward the hive bodies. Starting at the top, he riffled through each tray. He straightened up and gazed at the trees, facing away from them. Then he rotated, scrolling his head up and down. When he faced their direction, he stopped.

Sandy's throat dried. She tamped down the urge to cough. The man's head dipped slightly. She traced his gaze. Disturbed petals on the ground showed the dolly's tracks into the trees. She raised her head. He was staring right at them. He hollered, "Hey! I see you!"

Sandy stood still. Her heart thumped against her breastbone. She glanced sidelong at Hennig. His head dropped an inch, then he re-leveled his face and whispered, "Follow my lead."

Hennig stepped out from the behind the tree and sauntered towards the thin man. Sandy trailed him. She couldn't walk the stiffness out of her legs. He reached to his utility belt and unsnapped his holster's flap.

The thin man scowled. "Who the fuck are you?"

"We're from the government," Hennig said. "Conducting inspections." He continued his careful pace toward the man. Sandy copied his gait, keeping a couple feet off to his left. They'd gone over this scenario. He had phony credentials that would pass a cursory inspection. If worse came to worse, they'd imprison them, cover their heads in hoods, then set them free after they'd finished with the whole thing. The fat guy stood on the trailer's steel steps, glaring at her and Hennig.

"Bullshit," the thin man said. He twisted toward the fat guy and said, "Hey, the one with the tits must be Sandy Rhodes." He twisted back towards Hennig and pointed at him. "So, that would make you Albert Rhodes."

Sandy halted. She peered at the thin man. She didn't recognize him. But he recognized her, despite the baggy suit, which was designed for a man the size of a pro-basketball player. She looked to Hennig, who kept drifting toward the thin man. She chewed her lip. Maybe they were close to the plot Billy Bob assigned to Al. *Maybe.*

"Charlie," the thin man said, "get the motherfucking gun."

"Already got it."

Sandy grimaced. The fat guy must be lighter on his feet than he looked, because he was waddling towards them with a shotgun aimed at Hennig. She shifted her weight to her back foot. These morons were putting everything at risk.

Hennig extended his gloved left palm and said, "I have credentials." With his right he reached along his belt. Sandy ground her teeth. He had no shot at going for his gun. That left the nuclear option.

The fat guy stopped shoulder to shoulder with the thin man. He steadied the shotgun in the crook of his arm. "You go real slow now, mister."

Hennig took a couple of ginger steps towards the men. Sandy slipped closer to the trees. She couldn't believe Hennig's guts, walking right at the shotgun.

"Stop right there," the fat guy said.

"Okay," Hennig said. "Let's all stay calm."

Sandy hesitated at the edge of the trees. She'd killed a man, but Francis had been self-defense. But in a way, this was self-defense too. If they called the cops, it was all over. Everything. Every hope, gone. She whipped around and crashed through the low branches.

One of them shouted at her. The shotgun boomed. Pellets shredded through blossoms. The thin man said, "What the fuck?" She knew that Hennig had doused them. Now she had to hold up her end. She had seconds at best before they fired on him.

She dashed to the dolly and knocked the ceramic containers off of the wooden crate on the bottom. She grabbed the pry bar out of the duffel bag. She wedged the bar's chisel end between the crate's lid and its wall. *They recognized her.* The bar quivered in her hand, her actions agitating the bees within. She couldn't reconcile the fact that they'd recognized her with anything that he'd told her. But there was so much, she was afraid, that he hadn't told her. Or maybe he was lying to her.

She shook her head. She murmured, "No." They were saving the world. This was necessary. She wrenched the pry bar and the lid tore free. The bees filled the air around her. They coated her visor, blinding her. She raised her arms. *No. Be cool.* She forced herself to lower her arms, to keep her fingers loose. The suit would protect her. Bee by bee, her visor cleared. The swarm surged away from her. She stumbled to the edge of the trees in time to hear their screams. The shotgun went off again. She spotted Hennig, standing still. The men flailed, shrieked, went down under the yellow and black cyclone of enraged bees.

Hennig about-faced away from them. As he passed Sandy, he said, "Let's go."

"What about the bees?"

"Leave them."

To his back she said, "How … why did they recognize me?"

"They might dial 911 on a cell phone before the bees overwhelm them. We need to get out of here. Gather the things, I'll get the cart."

He hustled away from her. She stared at him for a moment before hurrying toward the dolly. He was right. But once they were safe, she was not gonna let him get away with blowing off her questions again. For damned sure he was gonna tell her everything.

Chapter Twenty-seven

Al gritted his teeth and stamped down the row. He'd thought his heel had ground his old man down to a grease spot.

His voice gaining volume like a dive-bombing horsefly, his old man said, "You're hopelessly lost."

Al swatted at his old man's accusation. His hand whiffed through empty air, then clipped the end of a long branch.

"You'll never find your way back. After sundown you'll freeze to death and some Spic will find your body."

"Shut up. I know what I'm doing."

His old man's voice corkscrewed upward around him as he said, "Hah! That's what you always say. Then you have to sell off plots of the family land to pay for your screw ups. One strip at time."

"Twice. I had to do it twice. And I'll buy it all back!"

"How? You can't even find your way out of this orchard. You haven't tended to the bees in days!" His old man's voice hovered a hair away from his left ear. "This is it, the screw up to end all screw ups. You finally killed the business, once and for all."

Al swiped at his ear. He shook his head, then cast his vision toward the horizon. In the distance, a deep plastic blue rose to the pinkish-white treetops. He pointed and yelled, "Hah!"

Al bared his teeth. His old man had no answer for that. Al hurried down the row to the tarps, then bulled his way through low branches until he found the seam in the blue plastic partitions. His old man remained silent as Al rushed toward the clearing, a limp marring his stride. He stopped and panted. The dirty white trailer, the flaky white paint on his hive bodies, he exhaled until he wheezed empty. He was home. Sort of.

He groaned while climbing the steel steps. He opened the unlocked door. He lurched into the kitchen, caroming from counter to counter. He snatched up the first empty glass and filled it halfway with tap water, then gulped the water down. He drank two more glasses, then he ransacked the cupboards until he found a box of cheese crackers. He stuffed his mouth. Shattered pieces of square crackers tumbled from his maw as he chewed. Muffled through the doughy wad in his mouth, he called out, "Sandy!"

110

He scrambled from room to room, cramming his mouth with more crackers. He found no sign of her, but in the smaller bedroom, he found his laptop sitting atop a strange wooden crate, a cord running from laptop to the adapter plugged into the wall socket.

He flung the cracker box onto the carpet. He went down to one knee before the crate and opened the laptop. The screen saver flickered away to reveal a single-spaced document. He read as fast as he could, scrolling down to the next page.

"Your manifesto," his old man said.

Al murmured, "Shut up."

"Might as well be a suicide note."

Al bit down on the sides of his tongue. He knew he didn't write this paper. But he could have. Some of it he recognized, cut from his blog and pasted to this screed. Whoever was setting him up meant for him to be dead, meant for the computer experts to analyze this 'manifesto' and pronounce it legitimate.

"It's got everything," his old man said. "Your failures as an athlete, as a businessman, and as a husband. Keep reading, I'm sure there'll be something about your failure as a father."

Al growled, "Shut the fuck up." He kept reading, and his eyes blurred over the section his old man predicted. He slowed his pace over the next paragraph, which described the tubes of pheromones in the crates. One formula provoked the killer bees' attack instinct, the other repelled them. He clicked on the link, which took him to a video which described the process he used to develop the killer brood.

"That's your voice on the video," his old man said.

Al couldn't argue. But faking that, that was kid stuff.

"You're so insane," his old man said, "that you've blocked all this crap out. Always wanted to be the hero. But the truth is, you've been a zero at everything you tried to do. Made you nuts. So you started doing all this crap … you seen it on those cop shows, where the firemen start fires, and the nurses causes emergencies, so they can swoop in and play the hero. You were doing the same thing, except that you screwed that up too."

"No."

"You ran all over tarnation thinking that Billy Bob took Sandy captive, and meant to sell her into white slavery. You built him up into some sort of criminal mastermind."

Al, scowling, nodded. "He tried to kill me."

"I'm not saying he's not dirty, but he's not Al Capone. And then there's the way you react every time–"

"Shut up."

"See what I mean? You're prone to paranoid fantasies, to blackouts, to blocking out things you don't want to think about."

Al stood up and left the room, hoping to leave the voice of his father behind. He stopped in the living room and gazed out the window. He whirled towards the door. He spotted the full-body white suit hanging beside the door. He'd never seen that beekeeper suit before. He snatched the cylindrical helmet on his way outside. He reeled down the steps. He stopped, closed his eyes, and took a deep breath. He pulled the helmet over his head. He blinked until his eyes adjusted to the dimming caused by the helmet's black visor.

A pair of huge bees whizzed around the helmet. He walked toward the hive bodies. He went through each tray. Killer bees crawled through every hive.

"See?" his old man said.

Al spotted his cell phone on top of the hive body. He grabbed it, called up the speed-dial menu, and punched in a code. "I'll prove to you that I'm innocent. I'll get the bastard to admit that he's framing me."

He breathed a sigh of relief when his call went to Billy Bob's voice mail. He roughed his voice, which was already muffled by the helmet, and said, "Boss, I found somethin' at the Rhodes' trailer you oughtta see." He hung up.

He waded a few rows into the almond trees and sat down, facing the trailer. He noticed three killer bees planting their abdomens against his mottled forearm. He didn't even feel their stings. He plucked one off his forearm. He crushed its head between his index finger and thumb. He tilted the helmet back from his head, enough to free his mouth, and he popped the dead bee in and chewed. He couldn't taste it. He lowered the helmet. He opened the all-in-one tool, selecting its biggest knife. His old man held his peace. Al snorted, then said, "Now we'll see."

Chapter Twenty-eight

Sandy stared upward. The ceiling, still distant and ethereal, had finally emerged from the darkest span of the night.

"I know you're awake."

Hennig's voice made her twitch. He didn't snore. Didn't fidget. She couldn't tell if he slept or lied awake, like her. "I kept waking up."

"You're thinking about those men."

"I … I keep thinking there must have been a better way."

He sighed. "I know I haven't been entirely forthcoming with you."

She bit her lower lip. This was it.

"Their deaths will more or less ensure the success of the plan," he said. Her heartbeat thumped in her ears. He slipped his hand over the back of hers, and locked fingers with her. She willed herself to relax, and to ignore the probability that he detected her excited pulse.

"Rising temperatures, summer heat waves, the melting polar ice caps and rising sea levels have not been enough," he said. "The increased frequency and the increased devastation of storms have not been enough. People do not want to give up their carbon-emitting lifestyles. And with China and India, along with the rest of the world, developing, and developing a taste for that carbon-emitting lifestyle that we have so brazenly modeled for the world for so long as *the* gold standard, we have reached that much-forewarned tipping point, where if someone does not do something drastic, it will be too late."

Her nod coaxed a slight creak out of the bedsprings.

"So what's the one phenomenon that always captures the public's attention?"

She flailed for the correct answer, her fervor thwarting her attempts to find the correct answer. "Um …"

"Scandal."

She frowned.

He chuckled. "You've said you don't see the connection between honeybee extinction and global warming, especially with the addition of the breed of killer bees."

"Yeah … keystone species, mutations …the dots don't quite connect. If you were targeting the pesticide companies, then the picture would be clearer."

"Precisely. The chain of logic is a bit muddled. If the picture was clear, the general public would quickly lose interest. Make the event puzzling, and it stands a better chance of holding their interest."

She clucked her tongue, then said, "But you said something about impacting the dinner table."

"Yes … that's the one-two punch. So as to generate a sensational scandal, a scandal that will capture the public's interest, and sustain that interest from the breaking of the story all the way through the investigation, the trial, and beyond."

She scowled. "Wait, what investigation? What trial? You don't mean …"

"I do mean exactly that."

Her muscles went rigid as her mind raced through the implications.

Still holding her hand, he shifted onto his side, facing her, and said, "Take it easy now. I've made my peace with this long ago."

"No. You can't."

"I must. Imagine the headlines, the constant babble of the talking heads, this story will spin out of control, go on forever, or, at least long enough so that global warming will be at the center of every discussion across the media spectrum, from the wonkiest of hard news shows, to the tabloids, and everything in between."

"So you're gonna let yourself get caught."

"Yes. You must be able to picture the progression. Celebrity scientist caught replacing honeybees with killer bees."

She cleared her suddenly thick throat. She managed a meek, "Yeah. They'll crucify you."

"Not so fast. I shall claim that I was simply doing the bidding of my corporate masters, performing a last ditch effort to divert the blame for CCD to Mother Nature. Survival of the fittest."

She tried to penetrate the shadows, to study his face, but the last vestiges of darkness obscured his features. "Wait, I'm confused …"

"Precisely. My erstwhile corporate masters will also be confused. They will scramble to disavow any knowledge of my activities."

"Oh."

He nodded. "Your average workaday person will not believe a word of the corporate claims. But the utter ridiculousness of my claims will cloud the issue, and the more clear-eyed of the media will not let this go unchecked."

"I still don't understand how this focuses attention on global warming. People will still think that pesticides caused CCD."

"That's where my all-out media blitz comes into play. I'll satisfy every review request, great and small, and in the course of this all-out media blitz, my secret will come out."

"Oh ... oh my god."

"Yes. At the first signs of media fatigue, I shall inject that particular strain of high-octane fuel into the story. And that will bring global warming to the forefront."

"And the trial, they won't find any evidence that you weren't acting on your own."

"Precisely. But the conspiracy theorists will howl that I'm being set up, that I'm a patsy. It will be the trial of the century."

"In the end, you'll be convicted."

"Of murder."

"But ..." Her thoughts swirled. She held onto the thread that troubled her most. "The scandal will fascinate the public, but they won't care about global warming."

"I disagree. People will argue about global warming. The time is ripe, another one of those tipping points. During the entire saga, should a hurricane land in a major American city, or a severe heat wave strike the South, or drought damage the crop yield throughout the Midwest, then the doubters will be forced, finally, to face reality. But should none of these catastrophes materialize, the investigation will finally pry the true studies out of the corporate vaults. Un-redacted, unedited, the public will finally learn the truth that the corporations have been covering up and propagandizing against for so long."

She endured the intrusion of a massive weight into her heart, then said, "What about you?"

"I am prepared to face the consequences. I assume in the end I'll either be murdered in federal prison, or kept in isolation from the general population for the rest of my natural life."

"No. Your plan …"

"I realize that it may seem like a long shot. But with the impact on the food supply caused by the temporary loss of honeybees, and the scandal, the public, across the entire spectrum of society, will no longer be able to ignore global warming. Something must be done. This is a chance that I'm willing to take. If somebody doesn't do something right now, it will be too late."

She couldn't help thinking about what would happen to her in the aftermath, and the shame of her own selfishness deepened her depression.

He patted her hand with his free hand. "Don't worry. You will not be implicated. You will be able to pick up where you left off. Finish school, follow your dreams."

She murmured, "There must be another way."

He released her hand and flopped onto his back. Enough sunlight crept through the blinds to blue the darkness. He cradled the back of his skull in his palms and let out a long sigh. "I'd be a liar if I claimed I wasn't daunted by the enormity of what lies before me. I'd be a liar if I claimed I hadn't been considering recent events, looking for a way to employ a particular substitute, a patsy."

"Who?"

He sucked his teeth. "Your husband."

She sputtered, "Al?"

His exhalation seemed to last forever, then he said, "I've been keeping his activities from you. I wished to shield you from further pain."

She narrowed her eyes. "What activities?"

"He appears to have had some kind of psychotic break. I'm sure you've already detected the warning signs. He's been roaming the countryside, wreaking havoc."

"Oh my god."

"He interfered with the capture of some illegal immigrants, assaulting their captors and setting them free."

She massaged her cheek with her right palm. She couldn't reconcile this strange act with Al's typical rants. Al was passionate about conspiracies, and especially agricultural issues. As far as she knew, he didn't give a fig about immigration.

"He managed to procure firearms, and then he ambushed a meeting of immigration officials. Fortunately, he didn't harm anyone."

"That's insane."

"Perhaps you didn't wish to acknowledge the warning signs, but cast your mind back. There must have been some indication that he was heading down this track."

She scoffed. She didn't have to work hard to remember all those nights he spent shut away in his 'study,' sitting in the dark, leaning towards the computer screen. Or the way he preferred to spend his days, mired in his 'systems,' which typically meant him working alone for hours, sometimes the whole day.

"And then there was a recent series of stressors."

She nodded. The business going under, his old man, then Mikey's death. More than enough to make him snap.

"That's not all, however."

She groaned.

"He opened fire on a meeting of beekeepers."

"Oh no …"

"Fortunately, he didn't harm anyone. They managed to subdue him. But then he somehow escaped from the police, and I understand they are in the midst of a manhunt."

Her eyes jittered back and forth. It was so difficult to process, it was so crazy, but worse, none of it seemed too farfetched. She could see Al doing all of it.

"The only reason I even contemplated using Albert as a substitute, as a patsy, is that he's almost surely going to be gunned down by the police, or by vigilantes. It is only a matter of time."

"I don't believe it … why didn't you tell me?"

He turned his head toward her. A ray of sunlight filtered through the blinds and sparkled in the green of his eyes. "Our relationship has been … unorthodox, to say the least. By the time we reached a point where I would tell you such things, I felt … you were … *are*, going through so much. I felt I'd be adding to your burden, telling you about him, and about my own endgame."

She sucked in a quick, harsh breath. "And you thought that you could substitute Al?"

He ran the backs of his fingers along her cheek. She closed her eyes, gave his fingers a slight nuzzle. He said, "I think, to perform a little self-analysis, that now that I am at the point of no return, that I contracted a case of cold feet, that I was chickening out."

She opened her eyes and gazed into his. He shrugged with one shoulder, then said, "Of course Al is not a suitable substitute. He lacks the requisite secret life, the discovery of which would fuel the scandal. It was a foolish notion, one that I've abandoned. I am resigned now, to my fate."

A tear trickled from her eye. She stared at the ceiling. She couldn't let him slip away, now that she'd finally found him. She couldn't let him go through with it. Al running amuck, she could see it. But if they threw Al under the bus, then people would say that Al had accidentally killed his own son. She gnashed her teeth. Her eyes widened. "It could work. Al, I mean."

He shook his head. "No. Not titillating enough for the public."

"Yes it is." She rolled onto her side toward him. "They'll blame him for Mikey's death. The sensational part will be an insane father causing the death of his innocent son."

He squinted. He lowered his voice to hush as he said, "No, I can't do that to the memory of your son."

"But it would work."

"It might. But no, I can't allow you to make that sacrifice."

"Listen, this would give my son's death, and his life, significance. I've been trying to do the hard thing, the right thing, the thing that will do the most good in the world, and this is it. If Al's gone crazy, and they're gonna gun him down like a mad dog, well, this will give his death meaning too."

His brow furrowed. His irises shifted back and forth, a habit she'd marked before. He was calculating, weighing and measuring. His eyes focused on her. "Are you sure about this?"

"The world needs people like you. After this, your cover won't be blown, and we can do so much more good. I'm sure about this."

"We'd have to throw suspicion off you. Stage things, as if you discovered what he was up to, and he held you prisoner. You'd have to go in front of the cameras yourself, and tell a story. The same story, every time, to the media, to the police, probably to the FBI. You'd have to denounce Albert publicly. Are you sure you're up to that?"

"Just give me that chance."

He exhaled through his nose. "We have to get to your trailer immediately."

She exhaled through her nose, set her jaw, then said, "Let's go."

Chapter Twenty-nine

The hum of an electric engine rose above the soothing drone of the bees and coaxed Al out of his stupor. Seated against a tree two rows deep into the orchard, he levered himself up to his haunches. He adjusted his helmet and peered through the black visor. A golf cart puttered up the rutted, grassed-over dirt lane. Pristine white jumpsuits and cylindrical helmets, just like his own head protection, disguised the cart's two occupants. The astronaut-fancy suits struck a chord in Al, but he couldn't zero in on it. Not Billy Bob, he knew that much. The cart looped around the clearing and disappeared behind the far side of the trailer, where the almond trees grew close. The engine died. The beekeepers hurried around the nose of the trailer and climbed the metal steps to the trailer's front door. One of them toted a black case. Al pulled himself to his feet.

Hennig drew his pistol and said, "You better let me go in first, just in case."

Sandy opened the screen door for him. Hennig pushed through the front door and lunged inside. A moment later, he said, "Okay, I think it's clear."

Sandy entered. He flattened himself against the open door, pressing it against the wall, and swiveled his head back and forth, gun in one hand, tool case in the other. Al's blanket and pillow remained neatly folded and placed at one end of the back-breaker of a couch. Some of the kitchen cupboard doors stood open. Through the helmet, she couldn't smell it, couldn't taste it, but the air seemed stale.

"The master bedroom," Hennig said.

She nodded and led the way, striding through the living room and down the hallway. The doors to the spare bedroom and the bathroom were closed. The master bedroom door was propped open.

Hennig took off his helmet and placed it on the floor, next to the tool case. She took off her helmet too. They worked fast. They employed grunts and curt gestures, a private language they developed while toiling amongst the hives. In less than two minutes he'd chained Sandy's hands and affixed the chain to an eyebolt screwed into a stud just above the head of the lumpy bed. They had to make the scene look forensically sound, in case the investigators turned out to be diligent.

Hennig straddled her, gazed down at her with his sizzling green eyes, and said, "Ready?"

"Yeah."

She pulled towards herself, tautening the chains. He grabbed each of her wrists. Between the two of them, they ought to be able to tear the eyebolt out of the wall with ease. The authorities would think she'd spent hours in the effort to free herself from her deranged husband's bonds.

Hennig's grip slackened. "Do you hear that?"

She stilled herself. She heard the rumble of an approaching vehicle.

He bounded off of her and scooped up his helmet. As he passed through the doorway, he said, "Don't make a sound."

She let her hands fall on either side her head to the lumpy mattress. She huffed a nonplussed laugh.

Al recognized the big black truck, which parked perpendicular to the trailer. Along with Billy Bob, two knuckledraggers got out of the cab. Al squeezed the handle of the all-in-tool. The short blade was no match for the thug's military-grade handguns. Thick clothing swaddled the trio, and veils draped down from their cowboy hats. Not a speck of exposed skin. Al guessed the bees weren't gonna be any help at all.

One of the spaceman-beekeepers appeared in the trailer's doorway. The gun thugs took aim at the beekeeper, who hailed them. Billy Bob commanded his goons to lower their weapons. The four of them congregated between the truck and the trailer, not far from the mini-maze of hive bodies.

Billy Bob said, "He called me, pretending to be one of my men."

Al winced. He reminded himself that his ruse worked well enough, luring Billy Bob out here. He just hadn't bargained on all these other assholes.

Billy Bob said, "That's what I figured."

Al concentrated, but he couldn't make out the beekeeper's response. Al ducked low and snuck from the trees to the closest hive body. He pressed his puffy palm against splintery wood.

Billy Bob said, "So he must be around here somewhere."

The beekeeper's words muddled indistinguishable. Al crept to the nearest opening between hive bodies and slunk closer to the men.

Billy Bob barked a smoker's chuckle. "I'll be damned. What the hell do I pay you fellas for?"

Al peeked over the rim of a hive body. Billy Bob whipped out his cell phone. Al scowled, then his eyes bugged. He scrabbled out his own cell phone and managed to switch the ringer just before the incoming call appeared on the phone's screen. The vibration was lost beneath the drone of the bees. Al drooped and exhaled a silent *phew*.

Billy Bob said, "Okay, show me what you gotta show me. I wanna get the heck outta here."

A gunshot made Sandy jump. Another shot, then the soaring buzz of raging bees followed. A man screamed.

Sandy pulled against the chains. She felt a little give, but the eyebolt held. She lifted her legs, gritting her teeth against the tightness in her hamstrings. She tucked her head and skidded her upper back along the bed. She worked herself onto her belly, her soles planted against the wall, her head near the foot of the bed. A barrage of gunfire sounded from outside. A couple of slugs plunked into the trailer's wall. She performed a version of a squat-thrust, and ripped herself free of the wall. She floundered off the bed and rushed to the window. A man wearing make-shift beekeeper gear, a veil descending from his cowboy hat, ducked by the tailgate of a big black pickup, and aimed a revolver at Hennig, who used the corner of a hive body for cover. Between them, two man-sized lumps, covered in a roiling black and yellow carpet of bees, laid motionless on the grass. Patches of bees roamed across the cowboy beekeeper.

Sandy lurched to the tool case. She found the keys and freed herself from the chains. She scanned the room, but her helmet was gone. It must've gotten tangled with Hennig's when he rushed from the room. She and Al kept extra gear in the spare bedroom. She dashed through the bedroom door and shouldered into the spare bedroom. She stopped and stared at the laptop sitting atop a wooden crate in the middle of the room.

Al watched the bees swarm over Billy Bob, seeking bare flesh to sting. The beekeeper's sporadic potshots kept Billy Bob pinned down by the truck's tailgate. The beekeeper edged down the hives, releasing more angry bees, which hazed the air.

The trailer's side door, the never-used one opposite the bathroom door, burst open with a metallic shriek and Sandy, wearing one of those space-age suits but no helmet, leapt through the door.

Her blazing eyes, her rage-red face, her sandy-blonde locks flowing behind her, mesmerized Al. There were no temporary steps under the door, so she plunged to the grass, tumbled, and popped up, her fingers curled into claws. She darted towards the beekeeper. Al launched into a sprint.

A blindside tackle knocked the wind out Sandy, her last gush of oxygen wasted on a frustrated scream. She and her tackler crashed into the grass. He mounted her, and she threw blind blows upward. One of her nails caught on a lumpy node and tore off. While she howled, the tackler forced something, a bag, a hood, onto the crown of her head. She punched and kneed, he woofed and panted. He pinned her right wrist and yanked the apparatus all the way over her head.

His weight left her. She pawed at the hood, felt the familiar texture, and she shifted the helmet so that she could see out of the black visor. Hennig flicked his hand outward and doused the tackler in the face with liquid pheromones.

"Oh my god," she said.

Despite the tangled, greasy hair, the overgrown beard, and the welts stippling his face, and every square inch of bare skin, she recognized Al. Then the bees swarmed his head. He exploded to his feet and ran between hive bodies, batting at his face. He toppled near the truck. The bees coated him, creating a man-sized bump on the ground, like the two between the hives and the truck, and the one beside the truck's tailgate.

Hennig loomed over her.

She looked up into his inscrutable visor and said, "You lied to me."

His head tilted a millimeter as he let out a slight snort. He pointed the gun at her face and said, "Take off the helmet."

"Was it ever about global warming?"

123

"You know your problem? You overestimate your own intelligence. Now take off the helmet."

"You were planning on setting up Al all along. Did you kill my son on purpose?"

"I can make death by bullet work, but, the bee venom carries a powerful anesthetic. The initial stings will hurt for a few seconds, then bliss will carry you away. Really quite humane, I think. Now, on the other hand, a bullet wound, I hear, is very painful. Now take off the helmet."

Over the manic buzzing of the killer bees, the truck's engine revved. Hennig's visor rotated toward the squeal of grinding gears. Dry old wood shattered. The truck's nose blasted through the nearest bank of hive bodies. Hennig raised his free hand. The truck's grill rammed into him and with a aluminum *crunch* plowed him into the trailer's wall. The truck's horn blared then died as the truck rolled backwards a foot or so and shuddered to a stop. Hennig slumped boneless to the ground.

Sandy spotted Hennig's gun lying in the grass. She snatched up the weapon and rushed to the truck. She opened the driver's door. Al, poor Al, sprawled across both seats. Bees circled above him and crawled over his body, searching for a patch of unprotected skin that wasn't already knobby from old stings.

She sobbed once. She waved the bees away from his eyes and mouth. She couldn't believe how stupid she'd been. She checked his jugular for a pulse. She couldn't feel anything over the reptilian scars, the damage from old stings, crowding his neck. She pulled the collar of his tee shirt up over his eyes. She whispered, "What did he do to you?"

Hennig groaned, then called, "Sandy ... Sandy, help me."

She snapped her head in his direction. She stalked toward him. His suit survived the impact intact. He lied on his side, his legs akimbo and motionless. He clutched his stomach with one gloved hand. His helmeted head swiveled back and forth.

His voice warbled as he said, "Put me in the truck bed. You'll have to drive me to the hospital." He aimed the visor at her and said, "Hurry!"

She scoffed. She couldn't believe his balls. "You got to be kidding me."

"You ... you don't understand. There's still time."

"You were gonna leave me here."

The helmet shook. "No. I wouldn't." The black visor fixated on her. The shock-note vanished, his voice steadied, as he said, "You tried to attack me. I thought you were turning on me. I see now that I was too hasty, that I didn't explain everything to you."

"You've been here. I saw Al's 'manifesto.' I saw the breeding video."

"I wasn't sure I could trust you with everything. But I am now."

"Take off your goddamned helmet."

Chapter Thirty

Sandy, alone in the waiting room, inhaled through her nose, as deep as she could, then exhaled completely. She let the tension melt from her jaw and her neck muscles. *Maintaining a constant façade is grueling.* She sank back in the fluffy chair.

She glanced at the magazines fanned over the coffee table in front of her. Her eyes stopped on the rectangle of the local newspaper, which lied outside the neat fanning, with its bottom half facing upward. She noted a column's headline. The killer-bee scare had descended below the fold, but remained on the front page. She supposed as long as rogue colonies of killers continued to migrate, infesting feral hives and evading eradication, their attacks would make the news. Interest in the ruined almond harvest had already faded, except in California, but the honeybee crisis had created a domino effect along the pollination corridor, devastating regional crops, and helping to keep the issue in the forefront of the public's mind. She wondered how many of those fanned magazines contained her story. Probably all of them.

She glowered. They didn't believe her at first, when she exposed Hennig's extreme leftwing politics. Then they found his state-of-the-art, self-sufficient, apocalypse-ready bunker. People were starting believe her story, the story he told her, the story she'd been so desperate to believe. She hoped that somehow he knew she'd twisted his plan back on itself.

She shook off the creeping stress. Nobody else knew the real truth, and nobody else ever would.

A nurse entered the waiting room and said, "Mrs. Rhodes?"

Sandy stood up.

The nurse smiled a row a perfect teeth at her. "I saw you on TV the other night. It's just amazing, the whole thing I mean."

Sandy sighed. "I'll be glad when the whole thing's finally over."

"I'll bet."

The nurse led her down the tranquil hall. The doctors had diagnosed catastrophic, permanent brain damage, the result of repeated doses of the toxic bee-venom. Sandy took the book deal so she could afford this place. So far, the first-class care seemed to be worth every penny. The nurse guided her into his private room. Al, seated in a wheelchair, raised his head. His disfigured grin stretched his scarred cheeks, crinkled the skin around his surviving eye.

Sandy smiled. She nodded to the nurse and said, "He's the real hero."

www.ingramcontent.com/pod-product-compliance
Lightning Source LLC
Chambersburg PA
CBHW060635130626
46555CB00002B/808